BALDUR'S BONES

Also by Mary Arrigan

Grimstone's Ghost

BALDUR'S
BONES

MARY ARRIGAN

An imprint of HarperCollins*Publishers*

To my husband Emmet, with love

First published in Great Britain by Collins in 2001
Collins is an imprint of HarperCollins*Publishers* Ltd
77-85 Fulham Palace Road, Hammersmith, London W6 8JB

3 5 7 9 8 6 4 2

Text copyright © Mary Arrigan 2001

ISBN 0 00 711154 1

The author asserts the moral right to be
identified as the author of the work.

Printed and bound in Great Britain by
Omnia Books Limited, Glasgow

Voices. The rat stopped scratching at the crumbly soil. Eyes darting, whiskers twitching, it shrank back from the pinprick of daylight. Freeze. Listen. Not the same voices as before. Lighter, not deep like the other voices that had driven long poles into the ground. Stopped now. The rat scrabbled and scratched frantically to bury the thing that had been disturbed, dragged up by the long poles. Deeper, it must go. Deep down where it must never be found. Deep, deep, back into the ground that had embraced it at the time of the screaming. Freeze! Those light voices again. Nearer now. Too near. Panic. Hatred and panic.

CHAPTER ONE

Click, click. Even the clocks sounded different here. Different and strange. Finn sat at the edge of the bed and looked out across the fields that stretched beyond the higgledy-piggledy arrangement of sheds in the yard below. Click, click. He rocked back and forth in time to the Humpty Dumpty clock that hung beside the wardrobe. Humpty-cruddy-Dumpty. Did they think he was some sort of little kid who could be fobbed off with baby stuff like that?

'Haven't you unpacked yet, Finn?'

Finn turned to face the stocky woman who stood at the door. Her face showed an expression of uneasy friendliness, as if she didn't quite know how to approach the boy. She pushed a wisp of grey-streaked hair behind her ear.

'I didn't hear you knock, Mrs Griffith,' Finn said meaningfully, knowing full well she hadn't knocked.

The woman smiled. 'Meg,' she said. 'You must call me Meg, dear. And no, I didn't knock. We're not a bit formal here. Do you want a hand with the unpacking?'

'No!' exclaimed Finn, swinging his legs across the bed to stand protectively before his assorted bags. 'No thanks. I'll get round to it soon.'

'Well, don't leave it too long, Finn.' The woman smiled again. 'I want you to make this your own special room. Put your own stamp on it.' She paused. Click, click, Humpty Dumpty broke the silence. 'Tea will be ready in half an hour,' she went on. 'You must be famished after your long journey.'

Finn pushed his thumb between his upper and lower teeth, just like he always did when he wanted his words to stay inside his head. Click, click. Finn began to rock on his feet to the rhythm of the clock.

'Right then,' said Meg, a look of helplessness crossed her face. 'I'll leave you to it, lad.'

Finn nodded, but said nothing as she withdrew, closing the door gently behind her. He looked at his bags and sat on the bed again. A sense of panic made his heart flutter. Everything he owned was in those bags. Once he'd unpacked and stored all his stuff in the alien wardrobe and drawers that stood waiting for them, then he'd be stuck here in this strange house with people he hardly knew. People who couldn't possibly want him. Click, click. That stupid clock. He fought back his panic. Why couldn't time just stand still? Better still, why couldn't time go backwards and pick up at the good bits? But no, click, click, it just kept on going. His heart fluttered again. Perhaps if he just took out his toothbrush. And maybe a clean T-shirt. Just a few things that he'd need. Leave the rest of his stuff packed. That wouldn't be so bad. Then he wouldn't feel trapped. Click, click. Finn scowled at Humpty Dumpty.

'Shut up!' he hissed. 'Shut up, you stupid clock.'

Humpty Dumpty smiled when the shoe knocked him from the wall. And he continued to smile as he crashed to the floor and his batteries rolled behind the chest of drawers. But the click, click had stopped. Finn listened to the silence for a few moments. Then he sighed and unpacked his toothbrush, the old Man United strip that he used for sleeping in, and a clean T-shirt.

CHAPTER TWO

'Hello. What are you doing in my patch?'

Finn jumped, his thoughts shattered by the clear voice that cut across this quiet place on the hill. He turned, frowning to hide his startled expression. The owner of the voice plonked herself on the grass beside him. Finn leaned away from her. She laughed and picked a blade of grass which she stuck in her mouth. Her red hair was caught in an untidy ponytail by a velvet scrunchy. Hundreds of freckles dotted her tanned face.

'You know you're trespassing,' she said. She laughed again, showing off teeth that her face hadn't yet grown into. Perfect teeth, Finn noted.

'No, I didn't know I was trespassing,' he muttered, getting up and rubbing the grass from his jeans. 'I just wandered here. No big deal. Keep your patch.'

'Oh, don't go,' the girl said, her smile switched off. 'I was just kidding.'

'Yeah, well I can find someplace else,' retorted Finn. 'There's a lot of countryside out there.'

'Come back,' said the girl. 'Are you always such a grumpy old thing?'

'Maybe I am,' said Finn. 'Whether I am or not, it's none of your business.'

'Oh, excuse me!' laughed the girl, her green eyes crinkling with humour. 'Someone has really rattled your cage. Get a life, sonny. Sit down, take that stupid scowl off your face.'

Finn hesitated. He wasn't used to such candour from someone he'd just met.

'What's it to you?' he asked.

'Look, I'm just making conversation here,' the girl went on. 'If you'd prefer to go and bury your miserable face someplace else instead of having a bit of a laugh with a charmer like me, then off you go. Your loss.'

Finn made to move away, but something made him want to stay around this outspoken girl with her green eyes and perfect teeth.

The girl noted his hesitancy. 'Look, we'll start again,' she said, spitting the blade of grass from her mouth. 'Hello you. Welcome to my patch. How's that? Does that warrant a civil answer?'

Finn smiled. 'It will do,' he said. He sat down again. 'What should I say now?'

'Oh, a grovelly thank you will do fine,' laughed the girl.

'I don't grovel,' replied Finn.

'No. I didn't think you would. Anyway, I don't like grovellers. What's your name?'

'You first,' muttered Finn.

'Ha! Like that, is it?' More tinkling laughter. 'Don't give anything away until you know the enemy. Cagey prat, aren't you? All right then, my name is Tara. Just fourteen. Not that age has anything to do with anything, but when you survive to fourteen you're entitled to brag. Now it's your turn.'

'Finn. And I can brag about being fourteen and a bit.'

'Finn,' Tara said. It sounded nice the way she said it, Finn thought. Then she giggled. 'Called after a bit of a fish then, are you? Could be worse, they could have called you Blubber or Anchovy.'

Finn frowned. Maybe he should have moved off after all. But he caught the mischievous gleam in her eye and knew she was just testing him.

'Better than being called after a lump of muck,' he said.

'What do you mean?' Tara asked.

'Your name,' went on Finn. 'Called after the Hill of Tara. Supposed to have been the home of the ancient High Kings of Ireland, but now it's just a big mound of muck and worms.'

Tara hooted with laughter. 'Oh my!' she screeched. 'There is actually a sense of humour under that sourpuss. There's a surprise. You'll do. Come on, I'll show you a special place.' She got up and stood before Finn. 'If you want to see it, that is.'

Finn got up. He was pleased to notice that Tara was half a head shorter than himself. She caught his arm and pointed down the hill. 'We'll go around by the lily pond and across to Cluain na nGall,' she said.

'Cluain what?'

'You'll see. Come on.'

Together they raced down the hill, arriving breathless at the bottom.

'How do you know this place so well?' Finn asked.

Tara shrugged. 'My dad owns all the land around here,' she said, making a sweeping gesture with her arm. 'Arthur Cavendish. Our ancestors owned loads more than this, but it's gradually dwindling. Dad sells some of it for sites for houses now, whenever we need the money – which is pretty often. The farming part doesn't pay all that much. My mother lectures in Dublin, at Trinity College. But for that Dad says we'd probably be on the dole. That's a laugh, isn't it? Years ago our lot were what you'd call "the gentry". All posh, and a heap of servants to keep the place humming.'

'Am I supposed to be impressed?' asked Finn.

'Lord no!' laughed Tara. 'Just pointing out how things can change. You can't take anything for granted. My old grandad would tear his hairy sidewhiskers if he thought that his son was depending on the earnings of a wife to hold the crumbling old place together. How about you? Does your mum work?'

Finn swallowed hard. He pushed his thumb between his upper and lower teeth.

'Finn? How come I haven't seen you around before? Have you and your folks just come to live here? Maybe

13

you've built on one of my dad's sites?'

Finn pressed harder on his thumb, conscious of Tara's frank curiosity. She stopped and looked at him. Finn withdrew his thumb and examined the teethmarks on it. 'You ask a lot of questions,' he said.

'Sorry,' said Tara. 'My mouth runs away with me sometimes. You don't have to answer my daft questions. My dad says that it's good to have a curious mind, but that too many questions can drive people mad. The people who are being asked the questions, that is. Are you being driven mad by my questions?'

She paused, caught a breath and continued before Finn could answer. 'Never mind. I won't ask any more. Come on. We're nearly at the pond. There are lizards in it. My great-grandma brought them back from some hot country and they've been breeding ever since. They're green and disgusting. At least that's what Granny Dob says. She lives with us. She says she's the last remnant of decency in the family. She thinks I'm a lost cause, but I know she adores me. Even when I tell her I'm going to be a rock star with tattoos and a pierced navel. I see more of Granny Dob than I do of my mother. Mum only comes home now and again. She has a flat in Dublin. Sometimes I stay with her, but I much prefer the wild countryside. When I'm not at school, that is. I go to boarding school. I hate it, but they wouldn't know what to do with me if I wasn't tucked safely away with the holy nuns. We're not Catholics, but Mum says that nuns give the best education. Why do you keep biting your thumb like that?'

Finn withdrew his thumb again. 'She's dead,' he said.

'Who? Who's dead?'

'My mother. She died three weeks ago. That's why I'm here. Mum's cousin is the only relation I have left. She has taken me on, herself and her husband. They're only distant cousins. But I'm not staying.'

Tara stopped and looked at Finn with concern. 'Oh my,' she said softly. 'And there's me prattling on and on. You must think me a right nelly. You poor thing—'

'I'm not a poor thing,' Finn snapped. 'I'll... I'll get by. When I've saved enough money, I'll be away from here.'

'What about your father?' asked Tara. 'Is he... is he dead too?'

Finn pushed his thumb between his teeth again. Suddenly this moment was turning into an ordeal. He felt drained. This silly girl and her silly questions.

'I've got to go,' he said.

'Oops, you're scowling again,' said Tara. 'Have I said too much? No more third degree. I promise. Don't go, Finn. It's nice to meet someone my own age in this godforsaken place. Everyone else is either away on holidays or brushing up on their Irish in one of those Irish language summer schools – all hoppy ceilidh dancing and bossy landladies.'

They continued in an uneasy silence for a while. Then Tara asked, 'What are they like? The relations who've taken you under their wing, what are they like?'

15

Finn stopped. 'There you go again,' he said with exasperation. 'I thought you were giving up on the questions. Look, I'll go home and write my autobiography. Will that suit you?'

Tara blushed. 'Sorry,' she said. 'I'm hopeless, aren't I?'

Finn was once more perplexed by such candour. Part of him wanted to flee, put as great a distance as possible between himself and this nosy female and her infernal questions.

'Old,' he said, before his feet could take flight. 'They're old, Meg and Bill. Their family is grown up. They came to collect me yesterday. They don't need someone like me in their house. They've finished with all that stuff. I wish they hadn't come for me.'

'Maybe they like having you,' said Tara. 'Though not if you're such a grumpalump. I certainly wouldn't want you clogging up my space if I was old and you were as grumpy as when I first met you.'

Finn looked at her and caught that mischievous gleam again. He gave a crooked grin. 'You're wired to the moon,' he said.

'Yeah, but isn't it more fun than being wired to a black cloud?' laughed Tara, running ahead.

She led him to the lily pond and they looked at the sleepy lizards. Then she took him through a grove of trees. Finn gasped when they turned a bend and were confronted with a flat wilderness. The stillness was the first thing that hit him. It was as if he had suddenly been clamped with earmuffs. Nothing stirred. The trees stood like silent sentries all around, casting cold shadows over the scrubby grass. Finn shivered and wrapped his arms around himself.

'What's this place?' he asked in a hushed voice. 'It's creepy.'

'Cluain na nGall,' Tara answered. 'Do you know what that means?'

Finn shrugged. 'Nope,' he said.

'*Cluain* means field,' went on Tara. 'And *Gall* means foreigner. This is the Field of the Foreigners. Dead foreigners,' she added as she moved into the scrubby grass. 'Underneath this wasteland is a whole bunch of dead foreigners.'

CHAPTER THREE

Finn gave another shiver. 'What do you mean?' he asked, following Tara.

She stopped and turned towards him. 'It's true,' she said. 'Way back, over a thousand years ago, when the Vikings used to come to Ireland, they'd sail their longboats down along the River Shannon, stopping at monastic settlements to help themselves to treasure. Cheeky prats. Well, some of them liked Ireland and decided to stay – Lord knows why, it can't have been for the weather.'

'I know all that,' put in Finn. 'We did all that stuff in history – about the Vikings coming to live here. Everyone knows that gangs of them settled in Dublin. They're still finding Viking things buried there. What's that got to do with this field?'

'I'm coming to that,' said Tara. 'Will you shut up and let the girl speak! At that time, Ireland was divided up among lots of chieftains who were all fighting one another for power. Some of them hired settled Vikings to fight for them as mercenaries – you know, soldiers who fight for money.'

'I know what mercenaries are,' said Finn impatiently. 'Will you get on with the story.'

'Yes, yes, keep your Velcro hair on,' laughed Tara. 'So, anyway, back then this whole region was governed by a chieftain called...' she paused. 'I can't remember his name.'

'Never mind,' said Finn. 'What happened?'

'This guy, whose name I forget, heard that the chief from a neighbouring region was planning an attack, so he hired some of the settled Vikings to protect his land. A fierce battle was fought here, right on this very spot. Loads of people died. The dead Vikings were separated from the rest and buried here. The Irish were buried in the old monastery churchyard beyond the village.'

'Why did they do that?' asked Finn. 'Why not bury all the dead together?'

'Because the Vikings weren't Christians,' replied Tara. 'They couldn't be buried in a Christian burial place, so they were buried on the battle site.'

'Bit unfair, that,' said Finn. 'They all died protecting the land. They should have all been buried together. That's stupid sectarianism.'

Tara shrugged her shoulders. 'What does it matter to them now?' she said. 'Does it really matter where your bones go when you're dead?'

'It's the principle of the thing,' muttered Finn.

'Ah, principle my eye!' said Tara. 'When you're dead, you're dead. No point in getting your knickers in a knot—' She broke off, realising that the subject of death was still a tender one for Finn. 'Anyway,' she said softly, 'that's why this place is called the Field of the Foreigners.'

'It's an eerie place,' said Finn. 'Cold.'

'Yes, but I like it,' said Tara. 'I come here quite a lot. It's as if... as if—' She broke off again.

'As if what?' asked Finn.

Tara looked at him with a shy expression on her freckled face. 'It's as if I'm drawn here,' she said quickly.

'You're what?'

'I know. Sounds crazy, but I can't describe it any other way. I feel drawn here. When I come and sit at the edge of this place, I get a strange feeling that I should do something.'

'Do what?' Her frankness continued to amaze him.

Tara shook her head. 'That's the frustrating bit,' she said. 'I don't know. I just sit here, feeling the silence – even though it's the scene of a bloody battle – but I don't know what to do. It's like when you go into a room for something and you forget what it is you're looking for. Does that ever happen to you, Finn?'

Finn was taken aback by the sudden serious tone of Tara's voice. It unsettled him. He preferred it when she was being funny and outspoken.

'That's what comes of spending time alone in weird places,' he scoffed. 'You should get out more, kid.'

Tara looked towards the wasteland. Neither she nor Finn spoke for a moment. In the trees some wood pigeons cooed softly. Who would believe, thought

Finn, that centuries ago men fought for a stupid bit of land here? And all for nothing. People are stupid. Death is stupid. He kicked at the grass and pushed his thumb between his teeth.

'You're doing it again,' said Tara.

'Doing what?' he asked.

'Pushing your thumb between your upper and lower teeth. Do you do that all the time?'

'None of your—' he began. But Tara's frank, open face made him stop. 'I hate my teeth,' he said in a rush. 'I have buck teeth and I hate them.'

'Is that all?' laughed Tara. 'Anyway, they're not buck teeth. You just have a bit of an overbite, that's all. Nothing wrong with that. In fact, it's quite attractive.'

'It is?' Finn looked at her intently. 'Are you winding me up?'

'No, you daft thing. I wouldn't wind someone up over something that bothers them. I'm not a total airhead.'

'At home, where I used to live, they called me Goofy.'

'Huh,' said Tara. 'I hope you beat the lard out of them.'

Finn shook his head. 'No. I believed them,' he said. 'Especially when my ma died.'

'How come?'

Finn kicked at the grass again. What am I doing, he wondered, telling this freaky girl with her posh accent and posh ancestry my deepest and most secret feelings?

I don't even know her. This place is doing my head in.
And yet it seemed OK to talk freely like this to Tara. It
was like letting years and years of steam out of a kettle.

'When they were burying my mother,' he paused.
Had he gone too far?

'Go on,' Tara prompted.

Finn took a deep breath before continuing. 'I tried to
grit my teeth to stop myself from crying, but my upper
and lower teeth wouldn't meet. I knew then, for
definite, that the boys in my class were right to call me
Goofy.'

Tara looked at him sympathetically, but she said
nothing.

'Stop looking at me like that,' Finn muttered.

'Like what?'

'Like you're feeling sorry for me.'

'Feeling sorry for you?' Tara snorted. 'Get real. I'm
just thinking what a soft nerd you were for taking them
seriously. You should have thumped them. I know I
would have.'

'Ha!' scoffed Finn. 'Thickhead louts, they'd have
knocked my teeth down my throat.'

'Then you wouldn't have your so-called problem,
would you?' said Tara. 'You big martyr. Come on, I'll
show you some of the bumpy graves.'

In spite of himself, Finn laughed.

Together they ran across the scrubby field.

'Have you noticed that it's colder as we go towards
the middle?' asked Tara.

Finn had noticed, but he felt it was up to him to keep level-headed.

'Maybe it just seems like that away from the shelter of the trees,' he said. 'They're huge, those trees.'

'Maybe,' muttered Tara.

'Shouldn't there be crops or cows or things here?' asked Finn.

'The grass isn't good enough for grazing,' replied Tara. 'And it couldn't be tilled for sowing crops.'

'Why not?'

'It's the bones, you see,' Tara went on. 'Nobody knows how far down they are.'

'Gross,' said Finn.

'Yeah,' agreed Tara. 'Anyway my dad says that, for years and years it's been a sort of unwritten rule not to interfere with this field.'

'Is there a curse on it, or something?' asked Finn.

Tara looked at him with a mixture of scorn and amusement. 'Don't be daft,' she said. 'That's storybook stuff. It's simply a case of letting these dead people rest. Would you want to tear up a place where people had fallen in battle?'

Finn shrugged. 'The bones are probably turned to powder by now anyway,' he said.

'Maybe,' said Tara. 'But it's still a resting place. Silent. That's why I like it. Can you not feel those calm vibes?'

Finn shrugged again. 'No. It's just a field as far as I'm concerned. A cold field with shadows, that's all. And a big rough circle in the middle.'

'Exactly!' said Tara, triumphantly. 'That big circle is the burial ground. It's nothing to be scared of,' she went on, as Finn instinctively took a step backwards. 'Come into the centre.'

They picked their way over the rough mounds.

'Now do you feel it?' Tara asked when they were standing in the middle of the circle. 'Do you feel anything?'

Finn stood very still. He was about to tease Tara for being the victim of an overloaded imagination when something made him stop. He caught his breath as an overwhelming feeling of urgency made every nerve in his body react with an uncanny uneasiness.

'Something—' he began.

'I knew it!' exclaimed Tara. 'I knew it wasn't just me. You feel as if you need to do something, isn't that it?'

'Stop putting words in my mouth,' said Finn. 'There's probably a very ordinary explanation. A magnetic force or something. Weird things can always be explained by science—'

'Don't give me that!' scoffed Tara. 'I'm telling you, there's something here that draws a person. Tell me truthfully what you feel, standing here.'

'Don't be so pushy,' Finn said, taking another step backwards.

'Sorry,' said Tara. 'But I have to know. I've never brought anyone here before. I need to know what you feel, that it's not just me. I'd go bananas if I thought it was just me.'

Finn looked at her earnest, anxious face and knew that he must hold nothing back.

'All right then,' he sighed. 'I do feel sort of drawn here. But I'm still not convinced—'

'Yes!' shrieked Tara. 'I knew it! I knew it wasn't just me. You feel it too. I knew from the first moment I set eyes on you that you'd be drawn to this special place. I just knew it.'

'Hold on,' said Finn. 'Let's not lose the run of ourselves here. It really could be just the power of suggestion.'

'Is that what you think?' Tara peered at him. 'Really and truly?'

Finn shook his head. 'No,' he admitted. 'It's a definite feeling. I'm not imagining it. I feel... I feel right being here. Right and kind of scared at the same time.'

It was at that moment that they saw the first rat.

CHAPTER FOUR

They watched in shocked silence as the creature clawed its way out of a mound of scrub. It was large, brown and menacing, its coat clinging in damp strands to its fat body. It looked at the youngsters for a moment before scuttling away towards the edge of the circle and disappearing into the grass.

'Yecchh!' said Tara. 'Where did he come from?'

Finn said nothing. He moved across to where the rat had burrowed its way out. He bent down and peered into the small cavity. Then he pushed away some of the earth.

'What are you doing?' asked Tara, her hands pressed to her face. 'There might be more of those disgusting creatures. I hate rats.'

'Come and help me,' said Finn, still pushing away the grassy soil.

'No way, I will not!' said Tara. 'Rats' pee can kill you. You can get a throat-gurgling disease from it.'

'The rat's gone,' said Finn. 'Look, there's a pretty big hole here. We might find something.'

'Like what?' asked Tara, tentatively making her way towards Finn.

'Dunno. Battle stuff, maybe.'

'Like there are swords and things just lying inches under there? Get real, Finn. That's just a filthy rat hole. Leave it.'

'No, wait,' said Finn, pulling away more sods of earth. 'There's something—'

'I said leave it,' Tara insisted. 'I brought you here to see the place, not to tear it up.'

'I'm not tearing it up, I'm—' Finn suddenly fell back on his heels. 'Oh my God!' he muttered. 'Oh my God! Oh no!'

'What is it?' cried Tara. 'Stop scaring me, Finn. It's not funny.'

But Finn just sat there on his heels, his stupefied face turning white.

'Oh my God!' he breathed.

'For crying out loud, you prat!' A note of hysteria was creeping into Tara's voice. 'Stop scaring me, do you hear?'

Slowly Finn turned towards her. 'Come and look,' he whispered. 'Come on.'

Tara half turned away, as if ready for flight, but her curiosity was stronger than her fear.

'If you're setting me up—' she began.

Finn ignored her and went back to gently shifting more soil. Tara stood over him and he backed on to his heels again to let her see.

Tara gasped. 'Is that... is that—?'

'A skull,' Finn finished her question. 'That's exactly what it is. A skull.'

Tara had her hands over her mouth to stop herself from crying out. She stared at the half-covered skull that grinned up at her.

'I think I'm going to throw up,' she murmured.

'Don't,' said Finn. 'It's just a dead head.'

'You're not going to touch it, are you?' Tara asked tremulously. 'For heaven's sake cover it up and let's get away.'

Finn gave her a cynical look. 'This is your special place, remember?' he said. 'You've been rabbitting on about your feelings and about the dead Vikings. Well, here's a dead Viking for you. You can chat with him first hand now.'

'Don't be so cruel,' snapped Tara. 'Crude and cruel. Cover it up. Now!'

'If you order me about like some servant, bossyboots, then I'll do exactly what you say not to do,' said Finn. Reaching into the gaping cavity, he gently drew out the skull. The two youngsters looked at it in silence. Tara jumped when a bunch of raggedy crows began an argument high up in the trees. The ordinariness of their cawing was a relief. She knelt down beside Finn.

'Poor sod,' she whispered. 'I wonder who he was.'

'A poor sod who copped it in battle,' said Finn. He gently brushed the soil off the skull. Then he began to laugh.

Tara looked at him with puzzled concern. 'What's so funny?' she asked. 'Have you gone mad?'

Finn shook his head. 'The teeth,' he said. 'Look at the teeth.'

Tara frowned and focused on the grinning skull again. 'So he has most of his teeth. That's not unusual – there were no gooey toffees and sugary drinks in those—' Then she realised what had made Finn laugh. 'His top teeth stick out,' she said. 'He has an overbite, just like yours.'

Finn was nodding. 'I wonder if he could fit his thumb between his upper and lower teeth,' he said.

'And did the other Vikings call him Goofy,' added Tara. 'Well, Goofy or not, put him back.'

'No, I don't think so,' said Finn.

'What?'

'I think I'm going to keep this Viking,' he went on, wiping away the rest of the soil and lifting the skull. 'Imagine, all those centuries ago there was someone just like me. A buck-toothed warrior. I'm taking him back with me.'

Tara backed away. 'You're mad,' she said.

'No,' said Finn. 'I'm dead sane. You brought me here. You made me feel part of all this. And I do. You talked about battles and Vikings. Now it's my turn. I'm taking a bit of all that home with me.'

He whipped off his sweater and carefully wrapped it around the skull.

'Finn,' began Tara.

'Don't try to stop me,' said Finn.

'I wasn't. I can see that you'd want a bony head that looks like you. Just... just be careful, that's all.'

Finn gave an involuntary shudder. 'I'm feeling cold without my sweater. Let's go.'

From the long grass, the rat watched.

CHAPTER FIVE

'What did you do with yourself this afternoon?' Meg asked. She was stirring something in a steaming saucepan. Something that smelled nice and reminded Finn that he was hungry.

'Nothing much,' he shrugged.

'Had a look around the village?' Meg went on, testing a slice of carrot to see if it was done. The juice ran down her chin and settled in the crevice between her chin and her plump neck. She wiped it with the back of her hand. 'Did you meet anyone?'

'Meet anyone?' Finn echoed. He shrugged again. 'Nobody to meet.' It was easier to fib than to get into a long discussion over meeting a girl on a hill who showed him a creepy place.

Meg nodded sympathetically. 'Pity it's summer,' she went on. 'If school was on you'd get to meet the youngsters at the Community College.'

'Yeah,' muttered Finn. 'Bad timing.' Bad time for Mum to die. She should have died in September so that I could make nice friends at school. Nice friends who'd make me happy ever after and glad to be here in this place. Yeah, right! Puke. He put his elbows on the table and cupped his face in his hands.

'Don't worry, you'll make friends,' Meg said. Now she was feeling the plates to test them for warmth. You'd never put a stew on to a cold plate. Mum used to say that. She made good stews, Mum did. Jesus, did you have to take her away? Deep breath. Grit the teeth that wouldn't meet. Think cool. A job sticking prices on things in the supermarket, maybe, and he'd save enough to be gone by the time he reached sixteen. A year and a bit wasn't all that long. Push those teeth and see if they'd meet. Deep breath. Mum.

'There's a soccer club,' Meg was saying. 'And Scouts. Were you ever a boy-scout, Finn?'

Finn shook his head.

'Well, maybe we can see about that,' Meg smiled. 'You'll get the hang of country life soon enough. Not as exciting as the life you've been used to in the city, mind. But there's a lot to be said for life in the country. You'll see. Before you know it, you'll have loads of friends.'

I have friends, Finn wanted to shout at Meg, with her wobbly chin and excruciating attempts at comfort and joy. I have a loopy, posh, over-the-top girl and the skull of a dead Viking with buck teeth. They're my friends.

Bill came into the kitchen and threw his cap on to a well-worn easy chair. The mark of the brim of the cap was indented on his sweaty brow, making his grey hair appear to be glued to his forehead. He turned and grinned at Finn as he washed his hands at the sink. 'Something smells good,' he said.

'You always say that, you old cod,' laughed Meg. 'If I served you boiled socks you'd say the same.' She glanced at Finn to include him in the banter, but he was fiddling with his knife, pressing a thumbprint on it and wiping it off again.

'Well, young man,' Bill said cheerfully, pulling out a chair. He put a newspaper on the chair so that his muddy jeans wouldn't dirty the gingham cushion. 'Had a look around, have you?'

'I was telling him that it won't be long before he makes friends,' said Meg, placing the pot of steaming stew on the table.

'And girls,' added Bill, winking at Finn as he shook out his napkin and spread it on his lap. 'With your looks, we'll be beating the girls from the door.'

Finn smiled politely as he held out his plate. He wanted to scream at these two old people to stop trying to humour him as if he were some pathetic child. With more force than was necessary he shook the ketchup bottle, spilling too much red sauce on the side of his plate. He stirred it through the stew and silently began to eat. He caught Meg's exasperated glance at her husband. Good, they were getting the message to leave him alone.

'How's the lamb?' Meg asked Bill. Then she turned to Finn. 'We have an out-of-season lamb,' she explained. 'Abandoned by his mother, the creature. If it was winter we'd have it in here beside the Aga. But it's grand out in the sunny shed with a soft bed of hay. We have to bottle-feed it.'

'You can come and see him after dinner, if you like,' said Bill.

Finn shrugged dismissively and said nothing. More awkward looks exchanged between husband and wife.

Later, in his room, Finn gently unwrapped the skull. He noticed the comfortable way it sat in his cupped hands. He took a tissue from the box Meg had left beside his bed and cleaned the remaining soil from the bony crevices.

He was so wrapped up in what he was doing that he was only vaguely aware of the furious barking of Jess the sheepdog outside in the yard. And, if he had looked out of the window, he'd have been surprised to see the dog, ears pressed back in fear, slink away from whatever had disturbed him.

'Who are you?' Finn said softly, tracing the eye sockets of the grinning skull with his finger. He put his thumb between the upper and lower teeth. 'A thumb-gap,' he said. 'Just like mine. Twins, me and you.' He reverently carried the skull to the high chest of drawers near his bed and placed it beside his rolled-up collection of old movie posters. 'There y'are, old warrior,' he laughed. 'I'll call you... I'll call you...' He paused. 'I'll look up a name for you,' he went on. 'A proper Viking name.' He jumped and quickly threw his sweater over his Viking when there was a gentle knock at the door.

34

He should have felt pleased that Meg had got the vibes he'd sent out about privacy, but it was a hollow victory because when she tried to please him, it only made things more difficult.

'Yeah,' he grunted.

Meg stuck her head around the door. 'I'm just off to Bingo,' she said. 'Bill will be back after he's seen to the cows for the night. Will you be all right? Go down and watch the telly. Watch anything you like. Bill usually just falls asleep anyway, so you needn't mind him.' She gave a slight shiver. 'Goodness, it's cold in here,' she said. 'Have you a window open?'

Finn could see her casting her eyes around the room. Thank goodness he'd hidden the Viking's skull. Her eyes rested on the untouched bags. She looked as if she was about to say something, but thought better of it.

'I'm not cold,' Finn said.

'Right, then.' Meg nodded and withdrew. Finn sat and listened to her feet shuffle down the stairs. The front door slammed. It had to be slammed, Finn knew, because it was old and warped, so you had to pull it really hard. The silence fell like a blanket over the whole house. Then he too shivered. Meg was right, the room had got much cooler. He looked out of the window to see if there was any visible sign of a weather change, but it was just an ordinary summer dusk. A breath of warm evening air caressed his face when he opened the window.

'Warmer outside than in,' Finn muttered. He closed the window and went downstairs to watch telly. If Bill was there, he'd just go out into the yard; he didn't have the energy or the desire to try to make awkward conversation with the old man. Any more, he was sure, than the old man would want to make awkward conversation with him. He was relieved to find the kitchen empty.

Outside, the hens had gathered together in a nervous huddle in a distant corner of the farmyard, too far away for Finn to hear their uneasy clucking. Later, when Bill rounded them up into their hut for the night, he was surprised at their panicky behaviour.

'Silly girls,' he muttered, glancing around to see what was disturbing them. 'Afraid of the shadows of dusk.'

If there was an extra shadow, he wasn't aware of it. It had been a long day and he just wanted to get a warm drink, and maybe have a snooze during the news.

Half-way through a quiz show, Bill came into the kitchen, followed by Jess, the sheepdog. He took off his wellingtons and padded over to the sink in his socks to fill the kettle. Finn jumped guiltily from the comfort of the shabby chair beside the Aga.

'This your seat?' he asked.

Bill waved at him to sit down. 'No, no, not at all. You just stay where you are, lad. Would you like a cup of tea?'

Finn shook his head. 'No thanks.' Jess came over and sat in front of him. Finn backed away.

'He won't bite,' said Bill. 'Jess is real friendly.'

But Finn kept his distance. Mustn't get close to anyone or anything here, after all, he'd be leaving as soon as he could.

'Who'd be a farmer, huh?' Bill went on. 'Twenty-six hours a day and nine days a week. And the only ones who get rich are the men in suits over there in Brussels.'

Finn smiled politely. He knew nothing about farming so there was really nothing to say. Bill rattled through the mugs in the press. 'Sure?' he asked, waving a flowery mug at Finn.

Finn shook his head again. 'Yeah, I'm sure,' he said. 'Thanks, but I think I'll just go to bed.' He glanced back at the telly to see if the current contestant had made it to the finals. The ads were on. Now he'd never know if she made it. Didn't matter. Who cared whether she won or not?

'Night, then,' he nodded to Bill.

'Good night, lad,' Bill responded cheerfully.

Probably delighted to have me out of his space, Finn thought. At the top of the stairs he paused outside his bedroom door. Chilly. He was pretty sure he'd closed the window. Must have forgotten. But when he entered the room he found the window shut tight. Stupid, draughty old house, he thought. Unsettling.

It was much later when he awoke from a dream-filled doze to see lights chase across his bedroom ceiling. He jumped, pulling the ear-plugs from his played-out Discman. Then he relaxed and smiled. Car lights. Meg back from her Bingo. He heard the front door slam again. Then muffled voices. Probably talking about him. He sighed as he tried to imagine the conversation: What did he say? What did he do? God, weren't we mad to take on a moody youngster like him? Finn thumped his pillow and pulled the duvet tightly around him. Such a cold night.

It must have been well past midnight when the second light woke him. Not a light really, more of a glimmer. Was Meg sneaking in to check on him? See if he'd done a runner? He pushed the duvet from his head. The figure standing by his bed was not Meg. Nor was it Bill. Tall, male, with grey clothes that blended with a grey face in the grey gloom. And a mouth which featured a familiar overbite.

CHAPTER SIX

'Get away!' Tara laughed. 'That's the most pathetic effort of a yarn I've ever heard.'

Finn stared at his shoes to avoid her scorn. 'It's true,' he said. 'He just stood there, looking at me.'

They were sitting on the grassy hill. Finn knew Tara would be there. All the way there he could picture her in yesterday's place waiting for him, and he wasn't disappointed. If only she'd believe him – she was the only one he could tell about his late-night visitor and all she could do was scoff.

'It was a nightmare, for heaven's sake,' went on Tara. 'And you deserve it, taking home that skull with you. That's enough to send bad dreams into anyone's sleep.'

'I'm telling you,' Finn snapped. 'It was no dream. I was as awake as I am now. I could see him as clearly as I can see you. Grey face, weird clothes.'

'And he just stood there looking at you?' Tara tri to pull back her grin when she realised Finn w serious. Finn nodded. 'Said nothing?' Finn again. 'And his teeth – same overbite?'

39

Finn bared his own teeth. 'Just like mine,' he said. 'You still don't believe me, do you? And yet you were the one who said you felt vibes in Cluain na nGall, weren't you?'

Tara shrugged. 'Vibes, yes,' she replied, looking intently at Finn for some glimmer of jokiness. 'But I draw the line at imagining ghouls in the night. No need to take it that seriously. Anyway,' she put her hands on her hips and shook her head, 'there's something we're forgetting here, isn't there?'

'What?'

'Well, cleverclogs, can you tell me how come you saw his face when we both know that his head and body are no longer stuck together? They're kaput, separated, no longer part of a unit.' Tara giggled. 'Did he pull his head out from under your bed, or wherever you've hidden it, and plonk it on his shoulders with a dab of Viking superglue that he's been carrying around in his shroud pocket?'

Finn grimaced impatiently. 'He was a spirit,' he muttered. 'Spirits don't need bones, they're different. Please believe me,' he added before Tara could respond with more gibes.

Tara shrugged again. 'If I say I don't believe you, you'll go grumpy. If I say I do and you laugh and say you were only kidding, I'll never speak to you again.'

'How many times must I tell you?' said Finn with an exasperated shake of his head. 'I was not dreaming. He was dead real.'

Tara laughed. 'Dead all right. OK, OK,' she added as Finn began to glower. 'I'm listening. So what did he want? Did he say anything?'

'No,' said Finn. 'He just stood there looking at me. Then Meg or Bill came upstairs and he just vanished.'

'You should have asked him what he wanted,' said Tara. 'What's the point in looming up in someone's bedroom and not saying why? You should have said something.'

'I was petrified,' exclaimed Finn. 'What would you do if a dead guy showed up in your room? Have a friendly chat? I don't think so.'

'Maybe he'll come again tonight,' said Tara, encouragingly. 'And then you can ask him. Personally I'd say he's after his head. Bet that's what it is – he wants his skull back. You've broken up his set of bones and he wants all his parts together again. I knew you should have left that thing in the ground.'

Finn gave an involuntary shiver. 'You could be right,' he admitted.

'Well, we'll wait and see,' went on Tara. 'There's no point in guessing. If he wants something badly enough he'll let you know.'

'Thanks,' muttered Finn. 'I'll really look forward to bedtime tonight.'

Tara laughed her tinkling laugh. 'Give him directions to my place. I'll sort the creep out.'

'Let's drop the subject,' said Finn. 'It's just making me more nervous. I'll try telling myself that you're right, that it was a dream, even though I'd swear he was really there.'

Tara jumped up and pointed down the hill.

'Let's go to the bumpy graves and see if he's hanging out there. He might be still looking for his head.' She began to laugh but stopped when she saw the doubt on Finn's face. 'Or would you be scared in case I'm right?'

'Scared?' Finn snorted, not very convincingly. 'No. But don't blame me if things get weird.'

As if, thought Tara. But she didn't say it in case Finn got the grumps again. Bad enough to have him jittery over a bad dream, but to wind him up would only lead to an argument and he might stamp off in a huff. She liked him and didn't want to lose his company, even if he was a bit of a grouch. They went down the hill in silence. When they came to the circle of trees, Finn hesitated.

'I don't know why we're doing this,' he said. 'He's hardly likely to be here.'

'Why not?'

Finn shrugged. 'Daylight,' he replied. 'Ghosts don't come out in daylight.'

'How do you know that?' laughed Tara. 'Just how many of these creepy ghouls have you met, Finn? It's vampires you're thinking of. Vampires don't hang out in daylight. Your Viking is not a vampire, is he? Were his teeth pointy or just plain goofy?'

Finn thrust out his jaw. 'Goofy,' he said. 'Told you – like mine.'

42

They fell silent again as they crossed over the uneven land. Tara stopped and looked at Finn. 'I didn't mean to use the word goofy,' she said. 'It slipped out. I told you, your teeth are not goofy, you just have a bit of an overbite.'

Finn smiled frostily. 'Doesn't matter,' he said, striding ahead resolutely. 'I don't really care what you call it.'

'That's the spirit,' said Tara. 'Come on, let's get this over with.'

As they neared the circle of Viking graves, Finn stopped suddenly. He held out his arm to stop Tara. She froze as she came to a stop behind him.

'What—' she gulped. 'What do you see?'

Finn took a step backwards. 'Look,' he said, pointing towards the centre of the circle. Tara fought back the urge to run and looked over Finn's shoulder. She gasped and clutched his arm when she saw the rats. They were moving stealthily through the grass, their curved backs forming a moving pattern of silent menace.

'Oh, gross,' she whispered. 'Where have they come from?'

'Same place as the one we saw yesterday,' said Finn. 'Something must have disturbed them.'

'Oh, I don't like this,' muttered Tara. 'They look like... they look like they're watching us. I'm out of here.' She backed away from Finn and then turned to run. Finn hung on for just a few moments. It seemed as if the writhing mass of rats, silent and still, was looking straight at him. His heart beat a faster rhythm because he felt, at that moment, an overwhelming sense of being the focus of something that made his blood freeze. He turned and raced after Tara, still conscious of the mean rat eyes that were watching him.

They didn't stop running until they were back on top of the hill. Tara flopped on to the grass, holding her chest.

'What was that about, do you think, Finn?' she panted. 'I've never seen so many of those... those disgusting things. Yeccchhh.'

Finn stood looking back the way they'd come. 'Like I said, something must have disturbed them,' he said.

'What? What could have disturbed them?' Tara sounded desperate. She stood up and touched Finn's shoulder. 'Do you know what I think?' she said.

Finn turned and looked at her.

'I think it's to do with that bonehead you took yesterday,' she went on. 'Before you found it, we saw a rat come out of the place where the skull was buried. And now this. It's too much of a coincidence.'

'Don't be daft,' scoffed Finn. 'What connection could there possibly be? Rats only breed, eat and sleep. An old skull wouldn't supply any of those things. No, something disturbed them. Maybe there's going to be thunder. They say that animals get restless before a thunderstorm.' He looked up into the sky, but there was just an eternity of sparkling blue. He shivered slightly and turned to Tara again.

'Let's get away from here,' she said. 'Suddenly it doesn't seem like my special place any more. It belongs to rats.'

'No it doesn't,' said Finn. 'Don't let your imagination run away with you, Tara.' But he was glad she'd suggested moving away, saving him the indignity of appearing scared. Which he was. That pattern of arched backs and glittering pinprick eyes was stuck in his mind like a recurring action replay.

'We'll go to my house,' said Tara, quickening her pace. 'I'm not coming to this spooky dump ever again. I need to be in a safe place. Oh, come on, Finn,' she said as Finn stopped and looked awkward. 'You can come too. It's no big deal. My folks don't bite, anyway Dad will be out mucking around the farm and Gran will probably be in the greenhouse torturing the gardener with her plans for changing everything around. We can chill out with some of the junk nosh that I keep in my room because my gran is a total health freak. Come on.'

'You sure?' said Finn doubtfully.

'Oh don't be so stuffy,' retorted Tara, striding ahead again. 'You're my friend and I'm asking you back for a drink. You won't have to recite poetry or bow to my old man, you know. Come on.'

Finn fell into step beside her as she led the way across a field, over a stream and into a grove of trees. The sun shone through the leaves, casting speckled shadows on the earthy ground. Neither of them mentioned the rats, each of them trying to dismiss the awful sight they'd left behind in the circle of trees. And Finn tried not to think of Tara's observation that the rats and the skull were somehow connected. He wished now that he'd never touched the wretched thing. Had he been dreaming last night? Can you have dreams so real that you can smell the earth from the thing that's haunting you? He grimaced as he followed Tara. There was so much churning around in his head right now, like coming to this remote place to live with two strangers, weird things going on and now this – following a bossyboots of a stranger to her fancy house where there would probably be poncy people asking him questions. And, of course, Mum. Always an image of Mum in there with all the extra baggage in his head. He took a deep breath and tried to push those teeth together again. Nope, they wouldn't meet. All he was rewarded with was a funny sound in his ears. He slowed down and looked at Tara's purposeful stride. He didn't want to do this, he wanted to turn and run to the house he'd have to call home from now on. Tara turned.

'Slowcoach,' she said. 'Look, we're there.'

No going back now, thought Finn. Another deep breath. Brave face, jutting jaw. Maybe, like Tara said, they'd all be out. He could have a quick drink and be gone before they'd get back. Tara stood until he caught up with her.

'See?' she said, pointing beyond the trees. 'The old homestead.'

Finn's eyes widened. 'It's big,' he said.

'Just a house,' muttered Tara. 'And full of cracks. We use buckets and buckets of Polyfilla to patch the cracks.'

Finn felt she was just saying this to humour him. He bristled slightly.

'No need to play it down on my account,' he said. 'I can see that it's a ruddy great mansion.'

'God, but you're such a deadbeat,' said Tara with vexation. 'I don't know why I've bothered to ask you back. No matter what I say you'll read something stupid into it. Perhaps you'd better go home and lose yourself in your own stupid misery. I can't be bothered trying to humour you and your pain-in-the-bum face any more.'

Finn was stung as he watched her flounce away, her bony elbows going like pistons.

'And another thing,' Tara turned around to shoot an insulting afterthought. But she didn't finish because her legs suddenly shot into the air as she tripped over a fallen branch. Finn dashed to help her up. When he saw her cross face, all the laughter that had deserted him for so long exploded in a frenzy of mirth. He laughed so much his eyes watered. He pulled her to her feet and then sank to his knees, doubled up with laughter.

'Not funny,' said Tara, scowling. 'And look, there's a dirty big grass stain on my jeans. I only got those new last week. Cost me a fortune.'

Finn's reaction was to roll over and laugh even more helplessly.

'You're right weird,' said Tara, the infectious laughter wiping the cross look from her face. 'One minute you're dragging your dreary mouth along the ground, the next you're laughing like a maniac. There are places for people like you, you looney.'

'Oh, Tara,' said Finn, sitting up and wiping his eyes. 'I'm sorry about your grass stain. And you're right, I'm being a total creep, feeling sorry for myself. You're the only one who can knock all that stuff out of my head.'

Tara folded her arms and looked down at him.

'Do you mean that?' she said.

Finn nodded as he got up. 'Hard to explain,' he said, 'but you seem to hit the right button to push away all the bad stuff that's—' His voice tapered. He'd said enough. Too much, maybe. He just tapped his head and gave Tara a bashful grin.

'Let's go then,' said Tara. 'Just don't let that mouth of yours go into a downward curve again. I hate it when you do that.'

'I'll try. So, what about that drink then?'

Neither of them noticed the stealthy stirrings in the grass behind them.

CHAPTER SEVEN

Up close, the house was altogether huge. Finn counted nine windows on top, along with four dormers on the roof. Virginia creeper and ivy covered the front wall.

'Nuisance really,' said Tara, following Finn's gaze.

'What is?'

'All that green stuff. It goes under the slates and Dad has to get someone to go up there and cut it back. Every year he says it's going and that makes Granny Dob go purple with rage. You see – we posh folks have world-shattering problems in big houses.' She looked carefully at Finn for his reaction. She smiled with relief when he grinned at her and said nothing. Good, he was learning. She'd make a human being of him yet. She led him around the back to a big, cobbled yard which was surrounded on three sides by stables.

'You have horses?' Finn asked.

'Just three,' replied Tara. 'Mine, Dad's and Granny Dob's. Mum hates horses.'

'What does Dob mean?' Finn asked. 'Granny Dob. What kind of a name is that?'

Tara shrugged. 'Never thought about it. She's always been Dob. Everyone calls her that. It's just a name.'

They were interrupted by two small dogs that shot from the open patio door like two yapping cannonballs. They flung themselves at Tara.

'It's OK,' she laughed, noting Finn's involuntary retreat. 'Bella and Ben, meet Finn. He can growl even louder than you two.'

'Thanks a bunch,' said Finn.

'Is that you, Tara?' a strident voice came from inside the patio door. Tara looked at Finn and wrinkled her nose.

'It's all right,' she said when she saw his dismay. 'She doesn't breathe fire or have snakes for hair. She's just an old lady. Come and say hello.'

Before Finn could object, Tara took his arm and guided him towards the window. He swallowed hard. He wasn't ready for this. Not yet.

Tara's granny was sitting at a small table near the window, her bony elbows on either side of the magazine she was reading. Her frizzy hair was a faded, grey-streaked version of Tara's. She put down the cup she was holding when Tara and Finn appeared.

'And who is this?' she asked, showing the same frankness as Tara.

Finn shuffled his feet, really wishing now that he'd fled.

'This is Finn,' said Tara. 'He's my friend. Finn, say hello to my dear old granny.'

Finn blushed and nodded at the old lady. She frowned and turned to Tara.

'I've told you not to call me that in front of people,' she said. 'It makes me sound ancient.'

'But you are my dear granny and you are old,' laughed Tara.

'Don't be cheeky, young lady,' said her granny. She turned her attention to Finn. He felt uncomfortable under her curious gaze. 'Aquarius,' she said. 'Certainly Aquarius. Are you an Aquarian, dear?'

Finn was lost. He looked helplessly at Tara.

Tara laughed and put her arms around the old lady's shoulders. 'Oh, Granny Dob, don't start into your stars bit. She does this every time,' Tara went on, looking at Finn. 'Every time she meets someone she has to slot them into their zodiac sign. As if any of that stuff mattered.'

'It matters,' said Mrs Cavendish. 'Place in time, child, place in time. Very important. Are you here on holidays, Finn?'

Finn's thumb began its involuntary journey to his teeth. Questions. Always questions. People always had to spoil things by asking questions, like vultures picking out your whole life from deep inside your head. Rat-tat-tat they'd spew them out – the same old questions. Who is your father? Who is your mother? What does your father work at? What does your mother work at? What do you think about? Which school do you attend? Who are you? Who are you? Who are you?

I don't fit in, he wanted to scream. And I don't quite know who I am and anyway it's none of your business.

He pushed his thumb further into the gap between his teeth and kept the words in.

'Finn has come to live on the Griffith farm,' put in Tara. 'He's only been here a couple of days, isn't that right, Finn?'

Finn nodded again, wishing his voice would come out with interesting and scintillating words that would make this lady gasp in awe. But nodding like a cheapo puppet was all he could rise to.

Mrs Cavendish looked at him with curiosity. 'The Griffiths? Decent people. And your parents? Are they with—?'

'Oh, hush now Granny Dob. Don't do your usual prying,' Tara interrupted, pulling Finn towards a panelled door on the far side of the room. 'Come on, Finn. Let's go to the kitchen and get something to drink. I'm parched.'

Finn glanced back at Mrs Cavendish, but she just gave a genteel snort, smiled to herself and returned to her magazine. Tara led him across a red-tiled hall, through an arch into a warm kitchen.

'It's Mrs Grady's afternoon off,' said Tara. 'So we'll have a bit of peace here. Granny never comes here except to give orders.'

'Mrs Grady?' said Finn.

'Housekeeper,' said Tara with a dismissive shrug. 'Been here for years.' She stopped and frowned at Finn.

'Say one grumpy thing about us having a housekeeper and I'll punch your nose.'

Finn laughed and put his finger to his mouth. 'Mmm. Lip zipped.'

'You get some juice from the fridge,' Tara went on, 'while I run up to my room and get crisps.'

Finn felt a slight sense of panic as Tara ran from the kitchen. What if Mrs Cavendish should come in? She'd start asking more questions and his words would get all mixed up. She disapproved of him, he could tell. You always know by the way people size you up if they disapprove, and she very definitely did. His clothes were wrong, his face was wrong, his teeth were wrong. He should never have come here. The only thing that stopped him from opening the back door and running was the thought of Tara. He didn't want to lose her friendship. He'd only known her five minutes, but already he was feeling the burden of loneliness lift from his shoulders. Come on, Tara. I hate it here on my own. Your granny does breathe fire and she does have snakes for hair.

As if in answer to his wish, Tara came bounding into the kitchen waving two packets of crisps.

'You didn't get the juice,' she remarked. 'I told you to get the juice from the fridge.'

'Sorry,' said Finn. 'But I wasn't going to go rummaging in a strange fridge. What would I say if your granny or father came in and saw me?'

Tara laughed. 'Wimp. Here, take these crisps while I grab the jug of juice. We'll go down to the orchard.

God, what's wrong with those horses?' She went over to the window that overlooked the field where the horses were. 'Listen to them, they sound like a whole bunch of banshees.'

Finn gave an involuntary shudder as the shrill neighing reached a crescendo. He followed Tara to the window. Minutes ago, when he and Tara had passed that way, the horses had been nibbling peacefully at the grass. Now they were galloping back and forth, their teeth bared with troubled whinnies.

'Do they normally do that?' he asked.

Tara shrugged. 'Not really, not all together like that. And certainly not so blasted loud. Something must have spooked them. Maybe a fox or something.'

Finn frowned, every nerve tense. He wasn't used to horses, but he knew there was something not right about the sounds coming from the trio in the field. Jeez, am I getting so paranoid that I think every weird thing is centred around me? Wise up, Finn.

'Shouldn't you see what's wrong?'

Tara shrugged again. 'Nah, they'll be OK.'

The frightened whinnying continued until Finn and Tara reached the creaky door in the high wall that surrounded the orchard. Then, as suddenly as they'd started, they stopped.

'See?' said Tara, with relief. 'Told you.'

It was cool under the apple trees. Eventually Finn began to feel more relaxed. Overhead, pigeons cooed and, in the distance, sheep were bleating. It was all so different from the city noises that he grew up with. Timeless, that was the word. If he could just stay here in this orchard for ever – no past and no future, just a contented now.

'Does your mother not have long summer holidays?' he asked as he crunched another handful of crisps. 'Don't universities have long summer holidays?'

Tara wiped her lip with the back of her hand. She screwed up her eyes and squinted into the distance, saying nothing.

'Tara?' prompted Finn.

She gave a snort and turned towards him. 'Told you, she comes and goes,' she replied. 'Likes to be in the city, near her work. And she travels, giving lectures and things at summer schools. It's OK,' she added when she saw Finn's surprised expression. 'It's just the way things are. She does her thing, my da does his and we all pull along nicely together. Pass me that jug, please,' she said in a different tone of voice. 'No talk of folks, all right?'

Finn nodded approvingly. 'Fair enough,' he said. 'Suits me.'

And so they passed the rest of the afternoon climbing the old apple trees that needed pruning. When they tired of that, Tara suggested rummaging in an old shed beyond the orchard wall.

Back at Cluain na nGall, there was a muffled rumble far beneath the earth. A rumble that could only be heard by the creatures that watched the two youngsters from the deep grass. A rumble that made them shuffle and stir with terror.

'What did you say?' Finn turned to Tara.

'Huh? I didn't say anything.'

'I thought you sort of squeaked,' replied Finn.

'Squeaked?' Tara snorted. 'I don't squeak, sunshine. If I want to say something I come right out and say it. Squeak? Ha! It's your brain cells straining to keep up with my brilliant company.'

She pulled open a stiff wooden gate at the furthest end of the orchard. Finn gasped. Through the arched doorway, a shimmering lake stretched away to a hazy outline of trees in the distance.

'Wow, mega!' he said.

'Lough Mór – Big Lake. You could fish there if ever you wanted,' Tara said, following his gaze. 'And swim, but it's a bit reedy around the edge. That lake stretches right across our land. You can just see the spire of the village church over on the right. Your place would be somewhere between here and there. Come on, let's have a look in the old shed.'

Finn followed her to an old stone building beside a run-down boathouse.

'This is where we keep all our junk,' said Tara. 'Just dumped here – forgotten stuff in a forgotten place. I like to rummage through all this and try to imagine what my family was like hundreds of years ago.'

'Dragons, I think,' said Finn drily.

Tara laughed her tinkling laugh. 'You mustn't mind

Granny Dob. I love her to bits and so will you when you really get to know her. She's just a big marshmallow coated with steel.'

'Yeah, right. Breaks your teeth before you get through to her.'

Tara laughed again and playfully punched Finn's arm. 'How dare you. Behave, or she'll feed you to Ben and Bella. She's dead proud of her ancestors who lived here – bores people to death when she gets going.'

'You mean she didn't marry into the estate?' said Finn.

'Lord no. It's thanks to Granny Dob that this is all Cavendish land. Her people had this place for ages. She was the last of her line and inherited it when my great-grandfather died. She'd married grandpa Cavendish by then. He was in the British army. They came to live here before Dad was born. And here we are, what's laughingly called crumbling gentry. Come on, let's look at the junk.'

There was so much stuff packed into the shed that it was hard to know where to begin. Tara pulled down a box and laughed.

'Look at this,' she said. 'My old Sindy doll. Her hair is all matted from being left out in the orchard. I used to have a playhouse there.'

'Funny shape for a doll,' Finn snorted. 'More like a mini version of one of those skinny models you see in magazines. I thought dolls were things you put in buggies.'

'Huh, easy to see you've no sisters,' said Tara. The words

had slipped out before she realised what she was saying, families being dodgy territory as far as Finn was concerned. She was relieved when he gave another dry grin.

'Not that I know of,' he said.

They pulled out chests and opened cupboards, examining the contents and exclaiming over the antiquity and beauty of things that had once been household items in another age.

'Some of these things belong in a museum,' said Finn, pointing to old iron pots and rusting farm implements. 'Wow! Look at this.' He pulled out a lance with the tattered fabric of a faded coat of arms hanging from it. 'This is deadly.'

Tara looked at it with only mild interest. 'Some ceremonial military thing from Dad's past,' she said. 'Lots of Cavendishes on the lists of dead soldiers going right back to Cromwell's time. Big waste. Did you ever wonder about the fact that all wars were started by greedy men after power and wealth?'

When Finn caught the mischievous glint in her eye he didn't rise to her feminist provocation. He grinned as he ran his hand along the shaft of the lance and caressed the discoloured metal of the pointed head. 'Bet this has seen some history in the making.'

Tara shrugged. 'Suppose so,' she said. 'Though personally, I must admit I'm not over-fond of sharp things at the end of long sticks. Look at these, though.' She opened a long box. 'An old croquet set. Dates from my great-grandfather's time. Can't you imagine them, men with hairy faces and women in flouncy skirts and stomach-bending corsets shuffling about the lawn with this lot. And some downtrodden little maid carrying out a big tray with a silver teapot and cucumber sandwiches for the gentry.'

'Just think if you'd been born then instead of now,' grinned Finn. 'You'd be one of the corsetted ones shuffling about with one of the hairy faces.'

'Yecchh,' snorted Tara. 'Can you see me fitting into that picture? I think not.'

'Oh, I don't know,' said Finn, trying to keep a straight face. 'Overbearing, posh, you have all the—'

'Shut it, creep,' put in Tara, wielding a mallet with mock menace. 'Another insult and you're dead meat.'

Finn responded by pointing the lance at her and they both giggled.

'I like it here,' said Finn, placing the lance carefully against the wall. 'I like old things; all dusty and cobwebby and smelling of years and years. Could we come here again?'

'Sure,' agreed Tara. 'We can make this sort of our special place. I could even hoard some of my foodie stash here and we could have picnics.'

'Wicked!' said Finn. Then he looked at his watch, shook it and looked at it again. 'What time is it?' he asked.

Tara smiled. 'Eight minutes to six. Nice watch. Does it not tell the time then?'

Finn held out his arm for Tara to admire the blue Velcro strap and big face of his watch. 'Digital. It's got a light and stopwatch as well,' he added. 'A state-of-the-art job.'

'And tells you what time it is in Bangkok and Timbuktu,' laughed Tara. 'But doesn't tell any time at all right now. Some watch!'

'Batteries are gone,' said Finn. He turned out the underside. 'See? It's inscribed, "To Finn on his 12th Birthday, with love from Mum".'

'Oh,' said Tara. 'Pretty precious then.'

Finn nodded. 'Too right. It's like—' he paused. Oh, what the hell. Tara was his friend. 'It's like I still have part of her with me as long as I'm wearing it.'

Later, as Tara walked him to the end of the long avenue, there was a distant whirr.

'Listen to that,' she laughed at Finn's puzzled expression. 'That's the church clock clearing its throat before chiming six o'clock. You'd best go through the town in case you get lost going back through the fields,' she said. 'See you tomorrow then?'

'Same time, same place,' said Finn. He went home feeling that maybe this summer might turn out OK after all. Maybe the black clouds in his head were starting to melt away. To his own surprise he began to whistle as he made his way along the main street. He hadn't heard himself whistle for a long time. Later, he thought, maybe later he'd put up just one of his old movie posters in his room.

That night the rats came.

CHAPTER EIGHT

Finn was wakened by the mooing of cows in the field behind the house. He didn't know it was troubled mooing, he thought it was just a normal farm sound and hoped that this racket wasn't going to be a nightly feature. He had just turned over and put his head under the pillow when Jess began to bark furiously in one of the sheds.

'This is all I need,' Finn groaned, clutching the pillow tighter around his head. Then he heard Bill's voice on the landing. His first thought was to hope that Bill wouldn't notice the rolled-up T-shirt Finn had stuffed on the top shelf on the landing. If the old man investigated he'd find the Viking skull where Finn had put it, in case of any weird repetition of last night. He still hadn't decided if it was a bad dream, as Tara said, or something more sinister. So, to be on the safe side, he'd hidden the skull in a place where he could easily retrieve it in the morning. Now Meg's voice. Surely this wasn't the usual nightly pattern?

'What can be disturbing them?' Meg was saying. 'Don't go out there, dear. It could be intruders. Let me ring the police.'

'It's probably dogs from the town,' said Bill. 'I'll frighten them off. Nothing to worry about.'

By now Finn was wide awake. He hopped out of bed and slipped into his dressing gown. 'What's wrong?' he asked, as he padded on to the landing. Meg looked at him with an apologetic expression.

'Oh, we've wakened the lad,' she said.

'What's wrong?' Finn asked again. 'Are the cows upset about something?'

'It's nothing,' said Bill. 'Go back to bed, the two of you. It's probably just a few dogs who've wandered far from town. I'll sort them out.'

But Finn could see that Meg wasn't convinced. She was rubbing her hands together in a gesture of anxiety.

'We don't get marauding dogs so long after the lambing season,' she said. 'I don't like this.'

Bill forced a laugh. 'You read too much bad news in the papers,' he said. 'Go on now, back to bed.'

'I will not,' said Meg, her voice raised with annoyance. 'I'm not going to lie in there worrying about you. I'm coming with you.'

Bill made an exasperated face and went towards the stairs, muttering as he went. Meg followed. Finn stood at his bedroom door. Should he leave them to it and go back to bed? After all it was none of his business. Let them sort it out, it was their farm. But something in

Meg's anxious expression made him decide to go after them.

In the kitchen Bill was pulling on his boots and Meg was lacing her scruffy trainers. They both looked up when Finn appeared.

'It's all right, Finn,' said Meg. 'Don't you worry about this. We'll see to it, whatever is disturbing those wretched creatures.'

Bill stood on a chair and carefully lifted a long object wrapped in cloth from the top of the dresser. Finn gasped as Bill unwrapped it.

'A gun!' he said. 'You have a gun!'

'A shotgun's a necessary thing on a farm,' grunted Bill.

'Listen,' put in Meg. 'The cows are quieter now. And Jess has stopped barking.'

The three of them stood in silence for a few moments. She was right. Bill gave his wife a triumphant grin. 'Told you,' he said. 'I knew it was something simple like a passing fox or a badger. Crisis over,' he added as he began to wrap the gun again.

The sudden slap at the window made the three of them jump. It was closely followed by another and another. Slap, slap, slap.

'Dear God!' whispered Meg. 'What was that?'

Bill strode over to the window, still holding the cloth-wrapped gun. When he pulled back the curtain, Meg and Finn cried out, backing away in horror.

'Rats!' shrieked Meg.

And so there were, dozens and dozens of rats. They piled on top of one another, their flimsy paws and white bellies pressed against the glass. Finn could hear them scuffling at the back door as if they were trying to tunnel through to the kitchen. He stood frozen with terror as more and more of them built up to a writhing mass. Now they were at the other window.

'Are all the windows closed?' barked Bill, jerking into action.

Meg nodded. 'I think so,' she said. 'What's happening, Bill? Why are they—?'

'No time for guessing,' said Bill. 'Check on the windows, just in case. One small opening and they'll all be in. Go on, you and the lad. I'll block the bottom of the door.'

Finn looked down to where Bill was pointing. Skinny, claw-like paws were now appearing under the door, scratching furiously at the splintering wood.

'Oh no!' he cried. 'It's me. They're after me!'

'Hush, dear,' said Meg, reaching out to touch him. 'They're not after you. It's just some freak thing that's driving them indoors. Could be the weather. Look, I'll draw the curtains so that we can't see them. There.' She swept the heavy curtains across, shutting out the stomach-churning sight of the rats.

Finn's head felt tight with tension. He wanted to stamp on those scrabbling claws, take Bill's gun and blast every rat to kingdom come.

'It's nothing to do with you, Finn,' said Bill as he

held a bundle of newspapers under the tap and began stuffing them into the gap under the door. 'Now go and check the windows as fast as you can.'

His calm order prompted Finn into action, racing after Meg. He could hear her wheezing as he followed her down the hall.

'I don't know what to make of this,' she was muttering. 'God help us.'

Together they recoiled when they saw a new batch of rats at the sitting room windows. They checked the windows to make sure they were securely locked and ran to the next room. It was the same at each ground-floor window – a mass of rats shutting out the inky night sky. Finn's breath was coming in short gasps as he tried to suppress the hysteria that was rising in his chest. It's me. I know it's me they're after. Those eyes. Those mean, glittering eyes, they're looking right at me.

'Don't look at them,' panted Meg, as if she'd read his mind. 'Just check the windows and don't look at them, the disgusting creatures.'

Bill was shouting from the kitchen. With heart in overdrive, Finn led the way back along the dark hall. Bill was crouched at the back door, desperately pushing more wet newspapers into the gap.

'Wood,' Bill gasped. 'This won't hold them back for long. I need bits of wood and a hammer and nails. Finn, lad, you'll find some in the cupboard under the stairs. Meg, you grab that bundle of papers under the cushion on my chair and run them under the tap. They're gnawing at the rotten wood—'

'Oh I knew it,' put in Meg, raising her hands in despair. 'I've told you hundreds of times to get a new door. That old thing's been splintering for ages.'

'Will you hush, woman. No time for arguing,' snapped Bill. 'Let's get this blocked or we'll have more than a rotten door to contend with.'

Finn raced to the cupboard under the stairs and frantically riffled through the toolbox, spilling nails and screws in his haste. He grabbed at the laths of wood that were neatly bound in the corner and ran back to the kitchen. Meg was shuffling back and forth to Bill with rolled-up wet newspapers. Finn felt an overwhelming sense of guilt. Bad enough for the elderly couple to be stuck with me, he thought bitterly, without having all this thrust on them as well. While Meg took over moulding the wet papers against the gap, Bill selected bits of wood to hammer on to the base of the door. Finn watched helplessly for a few moments. Until Meg suddenly stiffened.

'What was that?' she whispered.

There was a faint, scrabbling sound coming from the sitting room.

'The chimney!' gasped Meg. 'They're coming down the sitting room chimney!'

'Burn them out!' shouted Bill, turning desperately to Finn.

Finn grabbed another bundle of newspapers and a box of matches.

'Take that old blackthorn stick that's behind the door,' said Meg. 'In case any of them got in,' she added.

Finn swallowed hard. He didn't want to meet any of these vermin head on, in fact he didn't want to leave the kitchen, but he couldn't let the old couple down. He grabbed the stick and ran. He took a deep breath before opening the sitting-room door. Soot covered the sheepskin hearthrug. The squeak was the first thing Finn heard, followed by a scuffling sound somewhere up the chimney. Another batch of soot descended in a choking cloud. In the light from the hall, Finn swept across the floor, the blackthorn stick under his arm as he fumbled to open the box of matches. Shouting to block out the menacing squeaks, he stuffed the newspapers into the chimney and set fire to them.

'Burn, you sneaky filth!' he cried. There was more scuffling and more soot came down. It got into Finn's eyes and up his nose, but it didn't succeed in putting out the fire. He screwed up more and more pages, stuffing them into the flames, thankful that Meg and Bill were the type to hold on to old newspapers. His mum would never have done that – it was straight to the recycling depot twice a week for Mum. Oh, Mum. Don't stop to think about Mum. Finn shouted all the louder and frantically shoved more and more paper up the chimney. Shielding his face from the heat, he pushed the fiery mass further up with the poker. The squeals were loud at first, but then they subsided. He stood back, but no charred bodies fell into the hearth. Had they escaped only to try entering somewhere else? To be on the safe side Finn threw some of the sticks that Meg had neatly stacked beside the coal bucket. It was satisfying to see them take the flames from the burning paper and ignite into a longer-playing blaze. That should fend them off, Finn thought. He threw in another bundle of sticks before going back to see how Meg and Bill were faring.

If he had listened he'd have heard the deep rumble that emanated from the shadows, a sound not so loud as thunder, but deeper. More threatening.

Bill was nailing the last lath across the bottom of the door. He eased himself up and put his hand on his back.

'That should hold them,' he said. 'That and the double glazing.'

Meg leaned against the table, her face tense with fear and exhaustion.

'I've never seen the like,' she whispered. 'Dear God, that's the most frightening thing I've ever seen. What's it all about? Did any of them get in?' she asked, turning towards Finn.

He shook his head. 'I've burnt them out,' he said with vehemence. 'I've left the fire alight with sticks so they won't come back. I'll check on it again in a while.'

'Good lad,' said Bill. 'We'd never have managed but for you.'

But for me you wouldn't have had this horrible visitation, thought Finn, but he just pressed his thumb under his teeth to keep the words in.

'Listen,' said Meg in a quivering voice. 'They're still gathering at the windows. It's as if they're not going to give up until they find a way in.'

The three of them looked at the crude laths across the bottom of the door. Now and then a claw appeared through a tiny gap. Finn looked away. He couldn't bear the sight.

'Maybe the light is attracting them,' said Bill. 'I'll turn off the main light and just leave one of the wall lights on.'

The dim light gave an added gloom to the atmosphere. Bill pulled his chair over to the door and kicked at any claw that tried scrabbling at his handiwork. Finn felt helpless, watching the old man whose back was stooped with weariness.

'Is there any other chimney they could climb through?' he asked.

'Only that,' replied Bill, nodding towards the Aga that was giving out a gentle heat. 'We had all the bedroom chimneys blocked up when we got the central heating in.'

'That range is on all the time,' added Meg. 'Summer and winter we keep it going. I cook on it. If they try that chimney they'll roast, the wretches.'

'Windows!' cried Bill. 'Any windows open upstairs?'

Meg's hand went to her mouth. 'You don't think—?

My God. Oh no,' she wailed, with tired exasperation. 'I can't take any more.'

'It's all right,' said Finn. 'I'll go check.'

Meg and Bill looked at him gratefully. 'Good lad,' said Meg. 'I'll put the kettle on. It could be a long night.'

Finn glanced into the sitting room and was satisfied to see the flames still dancing to ward off the creepy intruders. Then he ran up the stairs, making plenty of noise in the hope that it would scare off any rats that might be on the way in. The windows in the first two bedrooms were securely locked. Bathroom, fine. Landing, fine. No sign of rats. When he opened his own bedroom door, he gasped with horror. His window, like the ones downstairs, was a slithering mass of vermin.

'Get away!' he shouted. 'Leave us alone.'

'Me,' whispered a hoarse voice from the darkest corner of the bedroom. 'It's me they want, boy.'

CHAPTER NINE

Finn clutched the door, ready for flight, but mesmerised by the figure that was emerging from the shadows. Same strange grey clothes that merged with the grey face. Same overbite.

'You,' he whispered. 'It really was you who came here last night.'

A tired sigh emanated from the figure. 'Don't,' it said as Finn's hand went towards the light switch. 'It's my eyes, you see. Leave the shadows, boy. I can only function in the shadows and I have much to tell you.'

'Who are you?' whispered Finn, backing away from this tall apparition. 'Was it you who brought all... all those.' He gestured towards the window where the rats were now more frantic than ever.

'I'm afraid so. It's my head, you see. They've been sent to get my head.'

'Oh no!' groaned Finn.

'Don't go!' the figure pleaded as Finn turned to run. 'Please don't go. You're my only hope.'

'Excuse me?' said Finn, pausing in mid-flight.

'It's true,' went on the tall spectre. 'But that shall wait. The most important thing is not to let the rats get my head. You must protect my head, boy.'

Spook or not, his self-centred attitude annoyed Finn, knocked the scariness aside.

'There's the small matter of protecting the old people downstairs and myself,' he said. 'You don't actually need that head any more, do you? After all you're not really in a condition to wear it.'

The spectre smiled, his ghostly overbite making Finn slightly more comfortable with his presence. If fear was relative, then this goofy wraith was less menacing than what was going on outside. But the comfort was short-lived as the scrabbling and screeching at the window got more and more urgent.

'Can't you call them off?' cried Finn. 'Please call them off!'

The spectre shook his head. 'They are my cursed enemies,' he whispered.

'Oh great,' muttered Finn. 'What can we do? You must know what we can do.'

'Just don't let them in. They must not get in.' He sounded frightened.

'That's easy to say,' said Finn shrilly.

'Sshh, easy, boy. It's just a matter of time now.'

'Time? They'll break a window soon. Look at them, they're pushing and scratching like maniacs. Either the glass will break or the whole window will come in on top of us!'

'Daybreak,' said the spectre. 'Just hold them off until daybreak. Then you must move my head. Heed me, boy,' he went on when Finn groaned. 'You keep on doing what you've been doing – keeping fires in the chimneys and blocking all entries. But most important – protect my head.'

'Who are you?' Finn asked again. 'And why do they want your head?'

'I shall tell you tomorrow at dusk. Wherever you put my head, I will follow and tell you all. So much depends on you now, boy.'

'Finn! Finn, is everything all right up there?' Meg's voice cut across the weird conversation.

'What depends on me?' hissed Finn. 'What are you talking about? Please don't go!'

But the spectral figure was already beginning to merge with the shadows.

'Keep them out,' his voice came from a distance. 'Dangerous, very dangerous. They will kill to get my head.'

Then, with a last toothy grimace at Finn, he disappeared.

'Kill?' exclaimed Finn. 'Come back! Tell me.' But the only sound was the scratching of claws on the glass. Finn looked at the mass of bodies with fear and hatred. He ran to the window and shouted at them, making sure that the window catches were secure. Then he pulled the curtains across to shut out the watching, frantic eyes and twitching whiskers.

Daybreak, he thought, please let everything hold until daybreak.

Downstairs Bill was tapping the window to try and scare off the rats. Pointless. Waste of time. These are not your average rats. Bill drew the curtain again when he saw Finn. Meg was filling the teapot with boiling water. Her hand was shaking.

'Everything all right up there?' she asked again. 'I heard you shouting. I was beginning to think you'd been swallowed up. Come and have a cup of tea. We deserve a break after this awful thing. I can't think what's driven those creatures to attack like that. Weather, maybe.'

'They'll be gone by daybreak,' said Finn, dropping on to a chair. He was drained.

Meg and Bill looked at him with interest and he was sorry he'd spoken.

'What makes you say that?' asked Meg.

Finn shrugged. 'Just... just know they will,' he muttered.

'Well, let's hope so,' said Meg doubtfully. 'We'll report this... this plague tomorrow and make sure it doesn't happen again. Listen to them, the disgusting things. I just hope we've covered every way they could get in.'

'Think!' exclaimed Finn, stiffening suddenly. He didn't want any doubts. 'Is there any other way? They mustn't get in, they just mustn't get in! They're killers!'

'Shush, lad,' said Meg soothingly as she took three

mugs from the dresser. 'They won't get in. Everywhere is blocked, isn't that right, Bill?' She looked at her husband for support in consoling the almost hysterical boy.

'That's right,' he said. 'And if any of them did get in, by jingo I'd shoot them to kingdom come.'

'They'd kill us,' went on Finn, looking at the tea that Meg had put in front of him, but not making any move to drink it. Bill forced a laugh.

'Not at all. They're only rats, not snakes or crocodiles. Vermin, Finn. It's all part of living in the country.'

But Finn was shaking his head. How could he even begin to tell these two people what he knew and who had told him. They'd be sending for men in white coats to cart him off to a place with rubber walls. Bill wiped the sweat from his forehead and stood on a chair to put the shotgun and boxes of cartridges back on top of the dresser.

'Don't think we'll need this now,' he said. 'Everywhere is secure. Relax now, Finn,' he added as he stepped down and sat at the table. 'Like you said, they'll probably be gone by daybreak. Get fed up, they will, when they realise they can't get in.'

He reached across and placed a comforting hand on Finn's shoulder. The boy felt uncomfortable with the gesture and moved his shoulder out of range. If Bill was hurt, he didn't show it. He sighed as he spooned sugar into his tea.

'Drink up,' said Meg. 'You'll feel better after some tea.'

Finn said nothing, but pushed the mug away. Meg opened her mouth to speak, but changed her mind and began to sip her own tea. Finn rocked back and forth in his chair impatiently. How could they sit drinking tea when death was facing them through the windows? He wanted to run, but where would he go? It was better to be here with Meg and Bill in the dimly lit kitchen than be alone. If only he hadn't taken that skull. Tara was right, he should have left it alone. He sighed. No point in thinking like that; the deed was done and he was paying the frightening price.

'Maybe we should just go back to bed,' Meg was saying. 'To be on the safe side we'll put more fuel on the sitting room fire and leave the fireguard in front of it. Thank goodness we had that double glazing done last year.'

Bill was nodding. 'No point in sitting here listening to them scratching,' he said. 'They can't get in.' He yawned. 'I'm exhausted. Let's go.'

Finn looked startled. 'No,' he said. 'Please don't go. I think we should stay here, make sure—'

'No need,' said Meg, hands on the table to ease herself up.

Her scream caused Finn and Bill to leap to their feet. Meg had her hand over her mouth and was pointing to the bottom of the back door. The first rat was through, its skinny claws pushing through the splinters it had been gnawing. Finn froze again with terror. Bill seized the blackthorn stick that Finn had left beside his chair and smashed it against the rat, leaving the creature stretched across the 'welcome' mat. But no sooner had he done so than two more rats clawed their way in.

Bill flayed about with the stick. 'The gun!' he bellowed. 'Get the gun!'

Finn jerked into action, jumped on the chair and grabbed the gun and some boxes of cartridges. He thrust the lot into Bill's outstretched hand and took the stick from him. Meg had fetched a sweeping brush and, with cries of horror, lashed at the incoming rats.

'Quick, get out!' Bill ordered Meg and Finn as he raised the gun. Meg grabbed the still terror-struck Finn and pulled him towards the door to the hallway. The blast from the gun in the enclosed kitchen was deafening. The pellets ricocheted off the tiles and wall, causing the rats to fall and scatter. In a panicky bunch they retreated towards the door.

'Gotcha!' Bill grunted with satisfaction. From the hallway at the foot of the stairs, Meg and Finn breathed a sigh of relief. Bill's next blast drowned the rumble that vibrated angrily in the night outside. But the rats heard. They stopped, panic-stricken in their need to obey. Then they turned to face their human enemy.

Bill couldn't believe it when he saw them reforming.

'What the blazes—?' he began, fumbling to reload quickly. No time to wonder at this unnatural turnaround. A blast from a gun usually sent any vermin running. He blasted again. And still they came, slithering over the dead bodies.

'Up the stairs,' Bill called out to the other two. Together the three of them backed up the dark stairs, with just a faint light coming from the kitchen door which Bill hadn't had a chance to shut. Horrified they watched the silent, shadowy rats flow towards them. As Bill reloaded and blasted, Finn and Meg drove the survivors back with thumps from Finn's blackthorn stick and the sweeping brush Meg had grabbed. The loud blasts and the squeals reverberated around the hall and staircase, the bloodied bodies of the rats tossed like garbage against the walls. Finn could see that there was no way he and the elderly couple were going to hold out against this attack. He could also see that Bill was near to exhaustion. This isn't right! Those rats have no right to put these people through such terror. The scum. I hate them. With fear replaced by anger, he stood beside Bill, clutched the stick in both hands and gritted the teeth that could meet.

'Come on,' he grunted. 'You scrawny scum.'

By now Meg, Bill and himself had reached the landing, the tide of malevolence still sweeping along the hall and up the stairs. Thank goodness it was a narrow stair, Finn thought. At least it meant a slightly better control of the approaching rats. Blam! Finn ducked as Bill fired another shot, and instinctively bent his arm over his eyes to protect them from stray ricochets. More squeals, more blood, more bodies. And still they came. Finn began to sob in frustration with each swipe.

They're out to kill. Try not to look at their snarling teeth and red eyes, just keep on hitting out. Stay alive. Then he remembered the skull. The only way out of this was to give them the skull! Finn thought of the spectre's pleading, but being a spectre he was already dead, Finn reasoned as he swung the stick again. He was about to push past Bill and Meg and run to fetch the skull, when the surging rats suddenly stopped. All together, all at once. Dead still. Finn grasped the stick more tightly – were they about to pounce? And then he saw the finger of daylight come through the landing window and spread along the backs of the still rats. Silently they turned and, without a sound, swept back down the stairs and out of sight. The three terrified people on the stairs didn't move. Waited fearfully for something to happen. Then Meg sank on to the top step.

'What are they at?' she asked. 'What was that all about?'

Bill took the stick from Finn. 'I'll check it out,' he said grimly.

'Daylight,' said Finn, his voice sweet with relief. 'He was... I was right, I told you they'd go at daylight.'

Bill turned. 'I hope you're right, lad,' he said.

Together Bill and Finn crept downstairs to the hall, stepping over the bodies of the rats they'd hit. Except for more dead bodies, the kitchen was empty.

'They got away quickly,' said Meg, from the kitchen door. 'Unless...' She paused and looked back anxiously into the hall. 'Unless they're somewhere else.'

'No,' said Bill. 'They definitely came in here. We definitely saw them come in here, didn't we?'

Finn nodded. 'Every one of them,' he agreed. 'The whole mass of them came into the kitchen.'

'Huh, didn't take them long to get through that little gap,' went on Bill. 'Still, no point in speculating. Thing is, they're gone.'

'Gone? Thank goodness,' said Meg, venturing further into the kitchen and looking warily around.

Bill gingerly eased open the door and peered out into the early dawn.

'All quiet,' he said, breathing a great sigh and closing the door again. 'Come on, let's get those disgusting bodies out of the house.'

Together, Bill and Finn shovelled the dead rats into a plastic sack which they put into a shed across the yard for burial later that morning. When they returned, the kitchen smelled of disinfectant as Meg scrubbed away every trace of the intruders.

'Bed, I think,' said Bill wearily. 'Let's try and rescue what's left of our sleep.'

CHAPTER TEN

It wasn't until well past noon that Finn awoke. His bedside lamp was still on. He couldn't believe that he had actually slept – his last memory was making a cocoon of his duvet so that no part of him was exposed to whatever horror might come during the dawn. How different things look in daylight, he thought, as he pulled back the curtains. No marks or scratches on the window to suggest the awful attack the night before. The sunlight that filled his room made the ordeal seem almost like a dream. On his way along the landing he checked the skull to make sure it was safe. After breakfast he'd move it.

Downstairs Meg was mopping the hall tiles. She leaned on the handle of the mop when Finn appeared on the landing.

'I hadn't the heart to call you,' she said. 'After all you'd been through I left you to sleep for as long as possible. You did sleep, didn't you?'

Finn nodded. 'You should have called me, Meg,' he said. 'You went through it as well. Why should I be different?'

There was the sound of voices outside. Bill came into the kitchen, followed by a man with a suit and a clipboard.

'This man is from the Environmental Health Authority,' he said. 'Come to see about the rats.'

'Thank goodness,' said Meg. 'You were very quick to respond.'

'We never take chances where rats are concerned,' the man said. 'Now, if you'll just show me where they got in.'

Bill showed him the gnawed gap at the bottom of the back door. The man bent down and examined it.

'How many were there?' he asked.

'Hundreds,' said Meg. 'Hundreds of them. They were crowded at the windows and trying to come down the chimneys. Hundreds.'

The man stood up and smiled with disbelief. He looked at Bill for a more realistic figure, but Bill was nodding in agreement with his wife. 'True,' he said.

The man looked at the gap again. 'And they all got in through that small hole and went out through it again?'

'That's right,' said Meg.

'Ah, come on, missus,' he said. 'Pull the other one. I can see how one or two might get through, but hundreds? I think not.'

'We killed some of them,' put in Bill. 'They're in the shed. Look, you can see where some of the tiles are cracked from the pellets I shot them with. Get the bag with the bodies in it, Finn,' he went on. 'We can prove that it wasn't just one or two as this man seems to think.'

Finn glowered defensively at the Environmental Health Officer. How dare he put on his superior smirk and doubt the word of Meg and Bill. He dashed across the yard to the shed and pulled back the heavy bolt. The bag was where they'd left it. It was open. And it was empty. Finn glanced nervously around the shed. Had they simply been injured and were lying in wait? But he knew they were dead. He and Bill had made sure they were lifeless lumps that they'd shovelled into the bag. Finn felt sick. When he arrived back at the kitchen, Bill looked at him questioningly.

'Well?' he said, looking at Finn's empty hands.

Finn swallowed and shook his head. 'They were gone,' he muttered.

'Gone?' exclaimed Bill. 'But they couldn't be! They were dead and in the bag—'

'I'm telling you, they're gone,' put in Finn.

The health officer was smiling again and shaking his head. Finn wanted to shake him, to make him believe the terrifying night they'd had. But what could he say? The more Bill and Meg argued with the man, insisting that there had been hundreds of rats, the more his expression made it clear that he thought they were a bunch of thickheads who'd got things thoroughly out of proportion.

'Look,' the man said finally. 'I'll leave you some rat poison. If this... this plague, as you call it, comes back again, just give them a dose of that.'

Finn looked at the small package the man had taken from his case. He wanted to scream with frustration. *That won't do any good. These are not ordinary rats. You've got to believe us, to help us.* But the words wouldn't come. He watched, thumb under his teeth, as the man drove away. Bill stood dejectedly at the back door.

'Doesn't believe us. Are you sure—?' he began, turning towards Finn.

'You think I'm making it up?' Finn snapped. 'Telling lies? Go and see for yourself.' Then he ran inside and up the stairs. He grabbed the wrapped skull and ran down through the kitchen.

'Finn, you haven't had anything to eat,' cried Meg. 'Where are you going?'

'Out,' he said.

'I'm sorry,' said Bill as Finn rushed past him. 'I wasn't doubting you, lad. It just slipped out. So much going on.'

'Doesn't matter,' muttered Finn, tucking the wrapped skull under his arm.

'What kept you?' asked Tara. 'I'd almost given up. You hadn't forgotten our meeting, had you? As if anyone could forget a meeting with *moi*!'

Finn said nothing. He was out of breath from running. Tara flopped down beside him on the grass.

'What's that you have there?' she pointed to the bundle Finn was carrying. 'Is it lunch? Meggy make a little cake for you, did she?'

'Open it and see,' said Finn, handing Tara the bundle.

'Yeeaagh! Gross!' she cried, throwing down the grinning skull. 'You rotten creep. Is this your idea of fun? Why are you carrying that thing around with you? You're a very sick person, you know. I'm not hanging out with you if you don't dump that bonehead.'

'Wait,' said Finn, wrapping the skull carefully. 'Don't go flouncing off again. I have a lot to tell you.'

CHAPTER ELEVEN

ᛏᚱᛌᛆᛒᛂᛁᚠᚹᛁᚴᛂᛏᚻᚹᛒᚤᛏᚿᚿᛁᚱᚴᛁᚠᚱᚹᛂᛒᛊᚠᚷᚿᛌᚴᚠᚷᚿᛌᚴᛂᛏᚷᛌᚴᛏᛌᚠᛚᛌᚾᛒᛌᛘᚻᚴᛁᚹᛏᛁᚱᚴ

Tara listened, sometimes putting her hands over her mouth. She poked at the bundle gingerly with her foot when Finn finished his account of the night.

'So, what are you thinking?' Finn asked. 'Say something.'

Tara looked up at him with an expression of disbelief.

'So. Here's this spook with his head stuck on – yes, yes, I know you told me he was a spirit and didn't need bones,' she held up her hand as Finn began to protest. 'But now you're telling me he spoke to you, right?' Finn nodded.

'Well,' continued Tara, smiling, 'would you ever explain how you understood this... this dead Viking. Did he sp—?'

'He spoke English,' Finn cut in. 'I didn't ask what language school he went to, did I? You don't tend to think of stupid things like that when a spook starts talking to you. You're just being awkward.'

'So you think that this thing's owner is up in your bedroom worrying about his head?' went on Tara.

'I told you. Didn't I tell you not to have anything to do with it? Now, see the mess you've gone and made of your own head. You'll have to get rid of that skull now.'

'No!' exclaimed Finn. 'Don't you see? He needs help. He said to put it in a safe place and that he'll come and explain.'

'Ha!' laughed Tara. 'And you think I'm going to fall for this? Sit around for some grey spook to come and have a cosy chat? I think not. You're on your own with this one, sunshine. Spooks, rats that will kill for a hunk of bone? Tara is definitely not interested.'

Finn put out a hand to restrain her as she stood up.

'Don't go, Tara,' he said. 'Please don't leave me to handle this on my own.'

Tara paused. 'Heavens, you really mean it, don't you? The mighty grumpalump is actually pleading. Things must be bad.'

Finn said nothing. He pushed his thumb under his teeth. Had he really pleaded? Maybe. But Tara was the only one he could tell. If she deserted him, he realised, he'd be more lonely and more terrified than he had ever been in his life. Tara stood over him, hands on hips. She wrinkled her nose while she turned things over in her mind.

'All right,' she said eventually. 'I'll go with you to put your spook's head in a safe place, but don't ask me to hang around until old greyface comes to get it, OK?'

Finn breathed a sigh of relief. At least that was better than nothing.

'So, where's a safe place then?' he asked.

'Oh, I can tell you that,' replied Tara, with a toss of her head. 'The safest place would be right back where you found it in that hole in the ground.'

'Oh, don't be smart, Tara,' said Finn. 'I was thinking, maybe that shed we were in yesterday—'

'Huh? You think you can offload your spooky stuff on my territory?'

'The shed is way down at the bottom of the orchard,' went on Finn. 'Nobody ever goes there, you said so yourself. We could lock it in there, protect it from the rats. It's so far from the house you wouldn't know if anything weird was going on.'

Tara wrinkled her nose again. 'Suppose so,' she said doubtfully. 'But at the first whiff of rats or spooks he's out the door, OK?'

They made their way along the route to Tara's house, keeping well clear of the Viking burial ground. However, Finn cast a wary glance in that direction. Feeling vulnerable and exposed, he would be nervous until he had put the skull in a safe place. If Tara noticed his anxious glance, she said nothing. She led him through high laurel bushes at the side of the house.

'Short cut,' she said. 'We wouldn't want to be meeting anyone who'd wonder what you have in that rolled-up sweatshirt. My granny, you see, she'd have it sussed in seconds. Says she's psychic. Gets vibes from the past, she says, but I don't go for that stuff myself.' Tara looked at Finn with a mischievous grin. 'She doesn't just have snakes for hair, but she has X-ray vision too. Runs into phone booths at any sniff of trouble and changes into red underpants and a vest with a big S on the front.'

Tara's humour always took Finn by surprise, but he was getting used to it.

'Yeah,' he said, 'I know that.'

Tara laughed loudly and ran ahead to the old shed.

Finn breathed in the evocative smell of old things that had pleased him yesterday. It seemed just right that the skull should be here. Safe. It must be put in a safe place. He looked around the crowded shed for a suitable spot.

'We'll have to put it into something,' he said. 'We couldn't leave it exposed in case those creepy rats get in. Is there anything like a box or something where we could hide it?'

They pulled things out and climbed over piles of bric-a-brac. From the top of a discarded iron garden table Tara let out a cry.

'Got the very thing! Look, there's a chest here. Big strong thing with a bolt. Will that do?'

Finn climbed up after her. 'Oh wow!' he said. 'Wicked!'

They heaved it down to the floor and pushed back the rusty bolt. Inside there were old discoloured papers which they emptied out.

'Phew, it's dusty,' said Tara, covering her nose with the top of her sweatshirt.

'It'll do,' said Finn. 'It's got a metal lining. Nothing could gnaw through that. Let's clean it out.'

'Clean it?' exclaimed Tara. 'Can't we just pop in dead Fred and get him out of sight. He won't mind the dust. It won't make him cough or sneeze, you know.'

Finn shook his head. 'No. It's got to be a proper place. He was once a person,' he went on, unwrapping the bundle and holding the grinning skull aloft. 'He used to have a face.'

'You're nuts,' said Tara. 'And I'm even nuttier to be helping you. Come on, I'll look around for something soft to cushion your mouldy pal. You clean out the chest. I couldn't bear to in case of spiders. I hate spiders almost as much as I hate rats. Wow!'

'What do you mean "wow"?' Finn looked across to where Tara had stopped.

She shrugged and shook her head. 'Nothing. Just a sudden shiver on the neck. Probably my nerves reacting to your pal there. Let's get him out of sight, eh?'

Finn sighed and ran his fingers around the teeth of the skull. Who are you? You don't scare me. Anyone with teeth like mine doesn't scare me. You want my help? You got it. No way – there's no way those blasted rats are going to get their slimy paws on you.

'Here's an old cushion,' said Tara. 'Will that do?'

'Brill,' said Finn. 'There, old fellow,' he said, as he ceremoniously lowered the skull on to the cushion.

'Let them try to get you now, the slimeballs. No teeth could gnaw through this.' He gave the top of the skull a gentle pat and closed the lid.

Outside, the leaves of the laurel bush shook. Just in one place. Glittering eyes were focused on the door of the shed. Eyes driven to malevolence through fear.

'See this old cabinet,' said Tara from across the shed. 'You can put your precious relic in here. Then I won't have to look at it.'

'Relic?' said Finn, carrying the chest to where Tara was holding the cabinet doors open.'

'Yes. I was in Italy with Mum two years ago and she hauled me around this cathedral in Bologna where they had bits of saints in silver containers and people were praying to them. Can you imagine? People praying to things like hair and kneebones and teeth. That must mean there are crowds of bald saints up there in heaven lurching around with no teeth and no knees.'

Finn chuckled. Plus the odd headless Viking, he thought. But he didn't say it. It wouldn't sound half as funny coming from him.

'Let's clean up,' went on Tara. 'Remember we said yesterday that we could have this as our special place?'

'You still want for us to come here?' asked Finn. He nodded towards the cabinet. 'Even with—?'

'Even with old deadhead here?' laughed Tara. 'Why not? It's not like he'll be tucking into any of our treats, is it?'

Finn frowned. 'You don't believe me, do you? You don't believe what I told you – about the rats and the ghost.'

Tara set about arranging two old chairs in the centre of the shed. 'That should do nicely,' she said, pretending not to hear. 'Two comfy armchairs.'

'Tara? Answer me. Do you believe me or not?'

She turned and looked at him, indecision in her eyes. She shrugged. 'You're very convincing,' she said. 'You tell your tales like a real pro. But...'

'But?'

She shrugged again. 'Sorry, Finn. But you've got to admit it's a pretty hairy story. It's all too much. Rats – yeah, I can understand maybe a few rats seeming like a huge gang late at night. And as for himself over there getting excited about his old head – well, you'd just woken up from your night's sleep. You must have fallen asleep thinking about the rats we saw at the Viking burial place and the memory blew right up in your dream. It figures. Think about it.'

'I see,' said Finn bitterly. 'So I imagined all that went on? You're just as bad as that environmental health guy. Why don't you come home with me right now and we can at least sort out the rats bit. Meg and Bill will tell you the truth.'

'Oh look,' said Tara impatiently as she shook the dust from the cushions on the chairs. 'There you go getting all grumpy again. Can't we just forget all this weird stuff? Let's get this place sorted, OK?'

Finn felt his anger rising. She doesn't believe me. She thinks I'm a right eejit. I want to argue it out with her, Mum, but she has a better way with words than I do. Should I just stamp away? Then I'd lose her. Don't want to do that. Maybe it is a difficult story to take on board. Deep breath. Say nothing. Let things rest for now. He bit his lip to banish the rest of his frustration and silently helped her shift the old furniture about to make their special place more homely.

Soon they had cleared a space big enough for the chairs, a small rickety table, a frayed hearthrug, some chipped china, an elaborate candelabra and faded velvet footstool. Behind a bundle of discarded panelling they found a lacquered screen which fitted nicely around the chairs, making the space cosy. They draped two moth-eaten curtains over two poles which they leaned against the wall on either side of the window. The heavy fabric shut out quite a lot of the light, but the place certainly looked more homely.

'There,' said Tara triumphantly when they'd finished. 'Our very own pad, away from nosy, bossy adults. We can bring games and stuff here. Deadly. I'll get a load of candles from the house for that candelabra.' She looked at her watch. 'Hell! Look at the time. It's way past lunch-time. I'm starving. Come up to the house with me and we'll snatch a sandwich, Finn.'

Finn shook his head. 'I'm not really hungry,' he muttered.

'Liar,' laughed Tara. 'Come on. I'm getting fed up with your complex about my folks. They're just regular people, so come on.'

Finn was resolute. 'No. I just want to stay here. I'll wait until you come back.'

'Don't you even want to go back to your own place then?' asked Tara. 'Think they'll be looking for you?'

'No,' said Finn again. He didn't want to face Meg and Bill. He couldn't bear the thought of their worried glances and obvious discomfort in his presence.

'Shouldn't you ring them then? In case they're looking for you. I'll bring my mobile.'

'No! Look, will you go and get your crummy sandwich and leave me alone. I'll just do a bit more fixing up here.'

'All right, all right,' said Tara. 'Keep your hair on. You're so... so touchy. Are you going to behave like someone with nettles in your knickers for the rest of your life? Chill out, Finn. I'll bring back a sandwich for you. Though why I should be so generous, I do not know.'

Finn watched her from the window as she skipped away. He wished he could be like that. Nettles in your knickers. He turned that thought over in his mind and found himself laughing. Even in her anger Tara had the power to lift his cloud. His face felt better for the uplift of laughter and he turned to see what more he could do to make this place really special.

The rustle from a dark corner made him freeze. Rats? He instinctively ran towards the door, his heart pounding. He tried to shout for Tara, but his throat was too dry. He stopped when he heard the familiar, hoarse voice.

'Thank you, boy. Thank you for heeding me.'

The spectral figure was sitting in the darker chair, the one in the shadow of the screen.

Finn stood behind the other chair and looked intently at his visitor. The spectre leaned forward and put his elbow on his knee.

'I am Baldur,' he said. 'Hear my story.'

CHAPTER TWELVE

'Ham,' said Tara. 'With onions and mayonnaise. How about that, Finn?'

Finn blinked as the sunlight flooded the gloom.

'Shut the door!' he cried.

'What?'

'Oh no,' groaned Finn. 'He's gone.'

'What are you on about? Who's gone?'

'Baldur, the ghost who appeared in my room' replied Finn. 'He was here. He's told me the strangest story.'

'Ah, come on, Finn,' said Tara, thrusting the sandwich into his hand. 'I thought we were leaving all that stuff behind us. You must have fallen asleep—'

'Stop!' Finn waved away her words. 'I'm telling you, Baldur was here. He disappeared when you barged in, letting in the light. He can't stand the light. Says it hurts his eyes.'

'Well, I'm very sorry, I'm sure,' growled Tara. 'If I'd known you were entertaining your dead friend I'd have knocked. Will you get real, Finn. Eat your sandwich and you'll feel better. Hunger, you see, gives you hallucinations.'

'Just shut up, sit down and listen,' ordered Finn.

Tara opened her mouth to say something, but she was so gobsmacked by Finn's surge of authority, she meekly sat on the chair recently vacated by Baldur. Not that she knew this, and Finn didn't tell her.

'Baldur was a Viking,' he began. 'He came to Ireland with his raiders over a thousand years ago. He liked it here and decided to stay. At that time, Irish chieftains were fighting one another for land and power. They used to employ Viking warriors who settled here, like Baldur, as mercenary soldiers to fight in their battles.'

'I know that. I told you that ages ago, you wuss,' put in Tara. 'Irish and Vikings fighting against Irish and Vikings. Crazy. No wonder we Irish are nuts. You know, for someone who's just been chatting with a deceased guy you're looking pretty calm. Don't look at me like that. I'm listening, aren't I?'

Finn was looking disgruntled at the interruption. 'Well,' he continued, 'Baldur was taken on as a warrior by a Munster chieftain called O'Brien. He fought lots of battles. O'Brien liked him and trusted him. He made him Master of Arms – the highest post – for his bravery and loyalty. This caused a bit – no – a lot of jealousy from O'Brien's son, Lua. He was afraid that Baldur would take his place as the next chieftain. He was doubly worried because Baldur fell in love with the chief's daughter, Áine.'

'Ooh, a love story. Now we get to the interesting part. And did Áine love him?'

Finn nodded. 'She did. They wanted to get married. But it was decided that a foreign invader, although settled, was not a suitable partner for the daughter of a chieftain.'

'Who?' put in Tara. 'Who decided that?'

'Lua, mostly,' replied Finn. 'It was Lua who insisted on this to his father. The old man was easily convinced and forbade the marriage.'

'Well, isn't that typical?' exclaimed Tara. 'The old geezer and the stroppy brother decide. Didn't Áine herself have any say in this?'

Finn shrugged. 'I suppose that's how it was in those days. Women did as they were told. Pretty good rule, if you ask me.' He ducked as Tara made to punch him. 'Just kidding.'

'You've just had a conversation with a ghoul and you can make jokes? Can't have been very scary, huh? Go on,' Tara said. 'What happened?'

'That's the weird thing,' said Finn. 'He wasn't scary at all. I kind of didn't think of him as a ghost. Well, anyway, Áine begged and begged, but her father had more important things on his mind.'

'What could be more important than his daughter's happiness?' interrupted Tara. 'Stingy old prat. How could he even think of other things?'

'A battle,' replied Finn. 'Word came that his territory was about to be attacked by another powerful Munster chieftain. O'Brien was worried because he knew he didn't have as many men as his enemy. Baldur went to O'Brien and told him he could muster some extra

Vikings who had recently settled on the west coast. Though he told me that it was not so much the family and land that he wanted to protect, it was Áine. O'Brien was so pleased with Baldur's loyalty that he promised him Áine's hand after the battle.'

'And did it happen? Did the old man keep his promise?' asked Tara.

'Stop interrupting. The battle took place out there, in Cluain na nGall. Very bloody, lots of lives lost on both sides. But Baldur and his men proved to be stronger and—'

'And won,' Tara interrupted again. 'Good old Baldur. And he got Áine?'

'There you go again,' Finn said impatiently. 'Will you let me tell it? Yes, Baldur survived and he was real chuffed – now he was free to marry Áine. But, as he bent down to identify one of the dead, he was hit from behind. He swung around, but it was too late. He just had time to see his attacker's face before he fell.'

'Oh, no,' groaned Tara. 'Don't tell me he died.'

Finn nodded. 'It was Lua. As he swung his sword he told Baldur that he would never have Áine and never be acknowledged as a hero because he'd been hit from behind.'

'Hit from behind?' Tara interrupted again. 'What's that got to do with anything?'

'Mark of a coward,' replied Finn. 'Back then it was considered that someone who'd been hit from behind was running away from battle.'

'Well, that's a load of old rubbish, that is!' said Tara. She toned down her indignation when she saw Finn's impatience. 'Go on then.'

'With his life ebbing away,' Finn continued, 'Baldur swore to Lua that he might have split him from his loved one in this life, but that Áine would be with him in Valhalla – that's the Viking heaven – for eternity. But Lua sneered and told him that without a hero's funeral he would still be unworthy of Áine, even in the next life.'

'That's a rotten ending,' said Tara, not adding that it sounded like an imaginatively padded out story of the one she had told back at Cluain na nGall. Let Finn have his moment. 'Couldn't you come up with a better ending than that?'

'Me?' said Finn. 'I'm telling you exactly as Baldur told it to me. In fact if you hadn't barged in, letting in the light, he'd still be here and you'd have met him yourself.'

'Yeah, right,' said Tara, smiling.

'Come on, Tara,' muttered Finn. 'Why can't you believe me? I'm not some dreamy kid, you know. I never believed in this sort of stuff either, until the last couple of days. It's real, dead real.'

Tara wrinkled her nose and leaned towards Finn.

'At the risk of being boring,' she said. 'And I know I mentioned this before, but how come you could understand him? I can remember being brought to the Viking Centre in Dublin as a kid and being told that the settled Vikings spoke a mixture of Norse and Irish.'

Finn shrugged his shoulders. 'He spoke just ordinary

English. Look, no big deal. Maybe dead spirits can speak any language. Who knows? His spirit's been hanging around for a thousand years, he was bound to pick up the language in all that time.'

'Floating around listening to people?' laughed Tara. 'Creepy spy.' She could see that Finn was getting annoyed. 'OK, simmer down. I'll accept what you say. Anyway, eat the sandwich I went to the trouble of bringing you. And I've brought some juice as well.'

Finn snorted. 'I hadn't finished my story, as you call it. Baldur wants me – us – to do something for him.'

'Oh?' Tara was smiling as she got up from the chair.

Finn ignored her smile and went on. 'Since you like happy endings, we can help him to have one. Remember he said that he swore to Lua that he'd be united with Áine in Valhalla?'

'And Lua said that he'd have to have a hero's funeral to achieve that. I remember. I was listening, you know.'

'Yes. Well, he wants us to give him a hero's funeral,' said Finn.

'What!' Tara sank back into the chair. 'Run that by me again.'

'He wants us to make a funeral pyre on a raft, set it on fire and send it sailing on the lake.'

Tara didn't want to dash Finn's imagination again. She knew that he was carrying a lot of emotional baggage inside him, so if fantasy was his way around that then she wouldn't be the one to knock it. Besides, she liked his company.

'OK,' she said. 'How do we go about doing that then?'

Finn's face brightened. 'You mean you'll help me?'

'Sure,' grinned Tara. 'Gives us something to do. Bit of creative fun, huh?'

'Well, it's a bit more than that,' said Finn. 'There's a snag. A couple of snags, really.'

'Thought there might be,' grunted Tara. She should have guessed that nothing Finn thought up would be straightforward. Maybe she should have kept her mouth shut about helping.

Finn took a bite from his sandwich before replying. He looked at Tara for any sign that she was winding him up, that she'd agree to help and then laugh in his face. Could he really trust her? But if he didn't, then who could he trust? He couldn't do this on his own. And, more than anything he'd ever done, he wanted to sort out Baldur. He wasn't quite sure why this ghostly figure was stirring up an affection he thought he'd lost. After Mum's death, that department of his brain had shut down. But now, here he was about to carry out the wishes of someone who'd died a thousand years ago – because he liked him. Liked a ghost? Was this crazy or what?

'Go on, then,' Tara was saying. 'What about these snags?'

'Well, there's a time factor,' replied Finn, wiping a glob of mayonnaise from his chin. 'We only have until the next full moon – that will be the one thousandth anniversary of Baldur's death. If the ritual funeral isn't carried out by midnight on that night, then Áine will be lost for ever.'

'And the next full moon is when?' asked Tara.

'Night after next.'

Tara couldn't resist a smile. 'I thought you were going to come up with something verging on the impossible,' she said. 'So, we have until the day after tomorrow to make the raft. That's a cinch. We'll easily have it made by then. Few laths of wood tied together—'

Finn was shaking his head. 'There's more to it than that.' He hesitated, wondering if he should share the next two snags with Tara. Had he not tested her belief enough? She would either laugh at him or abandon him as a crazy loon. He swallowed hard and rolled up the crust of his sandwich, watching the way the remaining bits of ham were making a curling pink swirl against the brown of the crust. Tara was looking at him expectantly. Finn cleared his throat.

'It's the rats,' he said in a low voice. He waited for an explosion of laughter. None came. 'The spirit of Lua has charged the rats of Cluain na nGall with guarding the bones of Baldur so that he will never have his ritual funeral. That's why they came to the farm last night. They will do anything, even...' he didn't add 'kill' fearing that would be too melodramatic. 'They'll do anything to get that skull back, you see. They've been guarding it for a thousand years. Something happened to disturb the bones recently and Baldur's skull was dragged to the surface.'

'Until you came along and nicked it,' said Tara.

Finn nodded. 'I've no regrets about that,' he said defensively. 'If I hadn't, then Baldur would never get the girl.'

'"Get the girl",' now Tara did laugh. 'You make it sound like some old movie. OK, so we don't have to worry about the rats. Baldy – I mean Baldur – is safely ensconced over there in his ratproof chest. Any other snag?'

Finn shrugged. 'He was just telling me what's needed for the funeral rites when you opened the door. He can't stand—'

'Can't stand the light. I know, you told me. Anyway, if that's all, then we can simply look up what went on at Viking funerals and follow it as best we can.'

'So you're still going to help me then?'

Tara gave him a mock scathing look. 'Didn't I say I would? Now, where do we start?'

'There's a bit more,' said Finn. 'Baldur had got as far as telling me that there had to be a weapon with the skull. That's what shows he was a brave warrior.'

Tara mused over that. 'We should be able to find something,' she said. 'There might be an old bayonet or something in our attic. Would that do? Or we could make a wooden sword. Surely it's just symbolic, eh?'

'Yes,' began Finn. 'But,' he paused.

'But what? Will you spit it out instead of sitting there shuffling your feet.'

'But he has to be holding the weapon in his right hand.' There, he'd said it – the worst bit. Tara looked at him for a moment.

'Well, I don't know if you've noticed, Finn, but there was no hand, right or left, sticking out of that skull. Where does that leave us?'

Finn swallowed again. 'His right hand was dragged up at the same time as the skull,' he said. 'It's just under the spot where I found the skull. It's back at the Viking burial place, and we have to get it.'

Tara looked incredulous. 'Now I know you're making this up,' she said. 'There's no way you'll get me to go back to that place, love story or not. Are you out of your little bitty mind, Finn? You saw those... those—'

'Rats,' Finn finished her sentence. 'The same rats plus hundreds more that you think I dreamt about. And yes, whether you come with me or not, I'm going to get Baldur's hand.'

CHAPTER THIRTEEN

Finn blinked when they went out into the sunlight. It seemed like a lifetime since he last saw daylight. Well, several lifetimes had passed actually, he thought. Lots of lives come and go in the space of one thousand years. Tara had suggested that they might find the makings of a raft around her father's farm buildings. With her usual impulsiveness she was charging ahead. Finn broke into a trot to catch up with her. She smiled when he fell into step beside her.

'I don't know which of us is loopier,' she said. 'You with your off-the-wall tale or me for going along with it. Up to a point, mind,' she added. 'Only up to a point.'

'Which point would that be?' Finn asked with a wry grin.

Tara looked at him. If only he'd grin more often; his whole face changed when his mouth went up instead of down. 'Dunno,' she said. 'I'll tell you when I reach it.'

She led him beyond the house to a collection of farm buildings. Two men were talking at the side of the cobbled yard. They looked up when Tara and Finn approached. One of the men was carrying a briefcase and looked out of place on the mud and hay scattered about. He ignored the two youngsters and continued talking. The other man waved and smiled.

'Come to boss us about, Tara?' he said. 'And who have you got in tow?'

His plummy accent caused Finn to shrink back. Tara's father wouldn't consider him a suitable friend, just like the granny. He shouldn't have come here. Should have known there would be family about. Tara turned and caught his arm.

'This is Finn, Dad,' she said, with an encouraging smile. 'He broke out of a circus and I'm sheltering him.'

There she goes again, thought Finn. Always takes the wind right out of my sails by saying the unexpected. He looked at Tara's father to see how he was reacting. He needn't have worried.

'Good,' said Tara's father. 'We could do with a few circus acts around here. How do, lad.' He reached out and warmly grasped Finn's hand before Finn could thrust his thumb under his teeth. That was it. No questions. No superior glances. Just a plain handshake. Finn took a breath and smiled.

'Hello,' he said.

'Any old lengths of wood knocking about that we could have?' asked Tara.

'What for?' asked Tara's dad.

'A raft,' said Tara. 'We've got a dead Viking and we're going to give him a ritual funeral on a raft.'

Finn felt the blood rush to his face. He couldn't believe Tara was saying this. Mr Cavendish laughed. 'Try the far shed,' he said. 'Should be plenty of bits there.'

Then he put his hand on the other man's shoulder and they both headed towards the house. Finn turned to Tara.

'I know exactly what you're going to say,' she laughed. 'I can see your brains boiling through your eyes. Don't worry, I say weird stuff to my dad all the time. It's, like, a thing with us. Why should he think I'm actually telling the truth? It's not as if he'd believe a story like that, is it? So, turn down the back burner inside that grumpy head of yours and let's get on with what we have to do. Look, there's Stanley, Dad's farm manager. He'll know where we can get stuff. Hi, Stanley,' she cried. 'Any old pallets you could give us?'

Stanley rolled his eyes to heaven. 'What major construction is it this time, Tara? Last time it was a tree-house.'

'Yeah, well how was I to know the stupid tree was rotten?'

Stanley directed them to a shed where they found several slightly battered pallets. They picked out the best one, along with some broken lengths of wood from other pallets, some nails and a hammer. Tara took a coil of string that was looped around a hook on the wall. They dragged their finds into the yard.

'Now what?' said Tara. 'Take this lot back to our place?'

Our place. Finn liked the sound of that. It gave him a feeling of belonging, of not being alone any more. He nodded.

'Our place,' he said. 'Yep, that's where we'll take them. We can work there.'

Between them they hauled their loot back down through the orchard. Finn couldn't quite understand Tara's enthusiasm. After all, she didn't believe his story.

'You sure you want to do this?' he asked. 'It's not too late to back down. I'll understand.'

Tara put her hands on her hips. 'Of course I'm doing this,' she said. 'I said I'd help. This is cool. I can't wait to set the whole thing on fire and shove it across the lake. Dead cool.'

'Well, we have to make it first,' said Finn.

The sun beat down on them as they hammered and bound the laths of the pallets together in a crisscross pattern.

The glittering eyes watched them for a while. When the earth trembled ever so slightly under their white bellies and skinny claws, the creatures shifted anxiously again. The Master! Listen, obey. They turned and began their journey to Cluain na nGall. It was getting near the time. One of them stayed – to watch the boy.

'He's OK, your old man,' Finn said. He'd been thinking about how Tara and her dad were so alike –

same sense of humour, same laid-back attitude. 'It must be nice.'

'What must be nice?'

'Joking together and all that. Bet you talk a lot, share things.'

Tara tossed her head dismissively, 'I suppose. He's pretty OK, is Dad. Doesn't nag. Yes, I suppose we do talk a lot, make each other laugh. And we do heaps of things together. He hates it as much as I do when I go back to school. Anyway,' she went on. 'No talk of school and stuff. This is shaping up pretty well. What do we put on it, apart from old Baldy's head and hand and a weapon. Surely it needs more than that to make it a decent ceremony.'

'Well, Baldur was just at that when you arrived. Maybe he'll come again.'

'Maybe,' said Tara, trying to hide a smile.

'You'll find out,' muttered Finn. 'I know you'll find out I'm not making all this up.'

'Sure. Just tell him I've revised my invitation asking him to call me. No midnight calls in Tara's room, OK?'

They set about their work again, nailing lengths of wood in the opposite direction on the underside of the pallet.

'A saw,' said Finn, leaning back on his heels. 'We'll need a saw to make the edges even. I think I saw one among all the junk inside. Won't be a sec.'

He went back inside the shed and partly closed the door to keep out the light.

'Are you here?' he whispered when he'd taken the saw from its hook. 'We need to know a bit more. You can come out now.'

But nothing stirred in the shadows.

'Don't be scared,' Finn went on. Mum, I'm telling a spook not to be scared!

Still nothing stirred. With a last glance around the shed, Finn went out to join Tara.

As Finn sawed away the rough edges, Tara gathered up the offcuts into a plastic sack.

'What are you doing that for?' asked Finn.

'For the pyre, silly,' replied Tara. 'Can't have a pyre without things to burn. This old wood is dry as a bone, it'll light up at the touch of a match.'

'Good thinking,' said Finn, returning to his sawing. 'I'm dead chuffed you're in this with me, Tara. I'd have freaked out ages ago if I was on my own.'

Tara threw her hands up in exaggerated surprise. 'A compliment! Oh, lawsy me, Sir Grouchalot has paid me a compliment! Stand back, I think I'm going to swoon.'

Finn stopped sawing for a moment. 'Don't knock it, I don't often give them.'

'You don't often give anything that involves words,' said Tara. 'You know, if you hold too many words inside your head you'll explode. Big hole will open on top of your head and a whole load of words will spill out. Except that by then they'll just be a jumble and you'll be sorry you didn't let them out when they made sense.'

Finn didn't respond, just kept sawing. Tara muttered an uneasy 'Huh' and resumed what she'd been doing. But silence didn't come easy to Tara. She stopped and looked at Finn again.

'About your own father,' she began.

Finn frowned, didn't look at her. 'What about him?'

'Do you ever think about him?'

Finn leaned back. Questions. None of your business. Let me get on with my tomorrows. But then Tara disarmed him.

'I like you, Finn. But I don't want you to be a mysterious stranger. I'd like for us to share our thoughts. Granny says that I'm like an open book – I let it all hang out. I wouldn't expect you to be like that, but you should release a little bit of yourself.'

Finn's first reaction was to push his thumb under his teeth. Instead he worked on in silence. Tara shrugged and went on with what she was doing. Finn turned over everything she had said as he sawed. She likes me, Mum – came right out and said it. She really wants to know more about me because she likes me. But if I let out what I think, I might get hurt. Better to keep my thoughts to myself, keep people at a distance because then, when they leave there's less pain. Like when you left me.

He glanced up at Tara, her hair half out of the velvet scrunchy and hanging over her face. A warm feeling of friendship flowed through him. He took a deep breath.

'I never knew him. When I was a kid,' he began, 'I used to pick out men's faces. Everywhere I went I'd pick out a man and wonder could that be my father. Sometimes a particular face would stay with me and I'd make up things like going to football matches with him and macho stuff like that. Bit pathetic, huh?' He waited for Tara to laugh. She stopped what she was doing and pushed her hair behind her ear.

'That's not pathetic,' she said quietly. 'Not in the slightest. I think it was a very sensible and imaginative thing to do. I'd do the very same if it was me.'

'You would?'

'Sure. But I'd also have throttled my mother into telling me who my father was. Didn't she ever even give you a hint?'

Finn shook his head. 'Maybe I really didn't want to know. It was easier to fantasise. We didn't talk about it, Mum and me. I knew it pained her so I gave up asking when I was about six. Sometimes though...' He paused. Perhaps he was saying too much. But Tara was looking at him expectantly. 'Sometimes, when we'd have a row, I'd yell at her that I hoped I was like my father and not like her.'

She grinned. 'Cheeky prat. Tell me, though, do you still fantasise father figures?'

Finn smiled a secret sort of smile. 'No,' he said eventually. 'I moved on to greater things than gawping at ordinary Joe Soaps in the street.'

Tara's eyes widened. 'You did?'

Finn fidgeted with the saw, unsure what to say or do next. Another breath. 'It was during the time Mum was sick,' he began. 'It got that she couldn't sleep at nights, so we used to rent videos and watch them together. That was pretty expensive, so we found out that old movies cost far less and we started renting those. Mum really liked those.' He paused again. Tara said nothing, stayed very still. '*Gone with the Wind*, *Casablanca*, anything with the Marx Brothers, old musicals,' Finn continued. 'Really old stuff. We'd prop up the pillows on Mum's bed and watch them. Even when she was really bad and used to drop off in the day, she still insisted on an old movie. She said she could hear it in her dreams and that it took the dread away.'

'Dread?'

'She knew she was going to die,' Finn said simply. 'She wanted to die at home. And she did, right in the middle of *Seven Brides for Seven Brothers*. God, she really liked those old movies,' he went on, a faraway look on his face. He turned to Tara again. 'And that's where I got my fantasy fathers.'

'What do you mean?' asked Tara, her eyes full of pity.

'Please don't look at me with that pity,' said Finn almost vehemently. 'I'm handling it, OK? I didn't want this to come out as some tragic tale of woe. I must sound like a proper wimp. Should've said nothing. It was rough, yes, but we had good times even when she was sick, Mum and me. She's gone and I'm getting on with life. Have to. Made a promise.'

'What's this got to do with your fantasy fathers?' asked Tara. 'You said—'

'Oh yes. Ha! Well I used to find it far more satisfying to think of some of those old heroes as my imaginary dad. Gene Kelly, Charlton Heston, Burt Lancaster, all those ancient movie guys were lining up to be my fantasy father. Does that sound sick?'

Tara laughed. 'Depends on who you're telling. Not for revealing to a bunch of guys in the locker room. But I don't think it's sick. What about Groucho Marx? Laurel and Hardy?'

'Nah,' Finn grinned. 'Only heroes.'

'And now?' asked Tara. 'What about now, since you don't watch those movies any more?

Finn felt something cold and wet against his bare ankle. He leapt to his feet. 'Tara!' he screamed. 'They're back!'

CHAPTER FOURTEEN

'Come here, Bella.' Mrs Cavendish's strident tone shattered the intimate conversation. Bella barked and ran to his mistress's feet. 'What are you two up to?' Mrs Cavendish went on. Finn looked anxiously at Tara to see if she would give her granny the same answer that she'd given her father.

'We just thought we'd build a raft, Granny,' she said. 'To see if we could succeed in getting it to float on the lake.'

'You're not thinking of sailing in it, are you?' asked Mrs Cavendish, her voice filled with concern. 'You know you're not allowed on the lake without one of us with you, Tara.' She looked at Finn. His thumb shot to his teeth. *She thinks I'm a bad influence. She doesn't want Tara hanging out with me.*

Tara gave a loud snort. 'What sort of eejits do you think we are? Sail in this thing? No. We were just messing about with the idea of how primitive people would have got about on the water, so we decided to build a raft. Nothing to worry about, Gran. Just think, we're out in the fresh air and using energy. You can't argue against that. Of course, if you'd prefer, we could go into the house and watch videos or play computer games. Nerdy stuff.'

'No need for sarcasm,' said Mrs Cavendish. She came nearer to examine the raft. 'That's pretty well done. Of course you're going to need something to make it buoyant.'

'Buoyant?' said Tara. 'What do you mean, Granny?'

'To make it float properly, of course. Those lengths of wood won't stay up on their own, you know. You'll need buoys. You'll probably find some in the boathouse. A couple of those lashed on to the sides will make that thing float.'

Tara smiled and looked at Finn. 'We'd never have thought of that, would we, Finn,' she said, drawing the boy into the exchange. 'Good job you came along, Granny Dob. Would you like to stay and help us?'

Mrs Cavendish laughed. 'Good heavens no. I'm just taking these two for a canter before dinner.' She paused and looked at Finn. 'Come and have dinner with us, young man. You can ring Meg Griffith and tell her you're dining with us.'

'No, I, er,' began Finn, blushing with confusion. Dinner, questions, scrutiny. He'd die. But Tara clapped her hands.

'Magic,' she said gleefully. 'Of course he'll come.'

'Settled then,' said Mrs Cavendish as she turned towards the orchard. 'Come on, you two,' she called out to the two dogs and ambled away. 'I don't know what's got into those dogs. They've been jittery and whimpering all the way here. Anyone would think they were scared of their own shadows. Come along!'

She was still muttering to the dogs as she disappeared beyond the bushes.

'But I didn't say I'd stay,' Finn hissed at Tara. 'Neither of you gave me a chance to answer. I can't stay to dinner.'

'Why not?' Tara asked with surprise. 'It's only a plain old meal, for heaven's sake. It's not like the family silver will be brought out or anything. Oh, come on, Finn. Don't go getting all weird on me again, just when I thought you might be human. Stay. I'd really like you to stay. Mealtimes can be so boring. Granny reads the *Sunday Times* because she says it takes a week to get through it, and Dad reads some frumpy farming thing. I usually end up talking to myself. What do you say? For me?'

Finn felt himself being won over, in spite of his doubts. 'Are you always so good at getting people to do what you want?' he asked.

'Of course I am. I've made it into a fine art since I was three. I take it that's a yes then?'

Finn nodded. 'Suppose so.'

'Huh, gracious to the last,' said Tara. 'You could say thanks for the invite, or that you'd appreciate the nosh. Just kidding. Come on, let's get those buoys Granny was talking about.'

Finn was standing perfectly still, his head on one side, listening.

'Did you hear that?'

'Hear what?' Tara stopped on her way to the boathouse.

'A sort of low rumble, like thunder. Only...'

'Only what?'

'Only it didn't seem to be from the sky – more like on the ground. I'm sure I could feel it under me.'

'Huh,' scoffed Tara. 'Probably just a hungry-belly rumble. That's what you get for not having a proper lunch with me. Serves you right. Anyway, if it is thunder it must be far away. I heard nothing.'

Finn looked around uneasily. He took a deep breath and tried to dismiss his anxiety, telling himself not to let paranoia turn his nerves to jelly. But it wouldn't quite go away, in spite of Tara's warning to 'get that frown' off his forehead before he turned into a prune. When he heard the second muffled rumble he said nothing. Earthworks somewhere? A train in the distance? Tractor revving up? Rats, spooks, evil... Stop! He expelled his breath and followed Tara.

Mrs Cavendish was already sitting at the table when Tara and Finn arrived at dinner time.

'We always eat in the conservatory in summer,' Tara said to Finn. 'The sun makes the food look a bit better.'

The evening sun made everything look good, Finn thought. The big airy conservatory had just enough plants to make it look exotic. The table was set with red place-mats, glasses with stems and a basket of bread wrapped in a napkin.

Mrs Cavendish was sipping sherry and nibbling some small crackers. She was reading a magazine article about Picasso. Finn recognised the big photo of Picasso because Mum had a book about the artist. Some poppy seeds from the crackers fell on to the magazine and Mrs Cavendish would periodically lick her finger and pick up the seeds. Finn watched, fascinated, as she picked the seeds right off Picasso's face and popped them into her mouth. She just nodded at the two youngsters and continued reading.

'Hands washed?' she asked, without looking up.

Tara wiped her hands on her jeans and winked at Finn. 'Yeah, Gran. Clean as a whistle.'

The door squeaked open and Tara's dad arrived with a steaming tureen.

'Grub's up,' he said. 'Mrs Grady's special.'

'Dad! You say that every day,' laughed Tara. 'How can they all be special?'

'Because no two Mrs Grady dishes are ever the same,' replied her father in a dramatically hushed voice. 'Even things with the same name always come out different...'

'Don't exaggerate, my dear,' muttered Mrs Cavendish as she drained the last of her sherry and began to ladle out the stew. It smelled good. Finn realised that he was very hungry. Apart from the sandwich Tara had given him, he'd had nothing to eat all day. Meg had been very surprised when he had rung to say that he was having dinner at the Cavendish house. She began asking questions, as expected, but Finn had fobbed her off by saying that he'd to go, that dinner was ready.

Dinner was indeed a quiet affair. Mrs Cavendish continued reading and Mr Cavendish made some small talk before flapping open his *Farmer's Journal*. Finn smiled at Tara. This wasn't such an ordeal after all. Until Mrs Grady arrived in with the dessert.

'So, you're the young lad that's come to live with the Griffiths,' she said, peering at Finn. 'Shame about your mother, lad. You must be lost, poor soul. Aren't you lucky Meg and Bill took you on. Fine people. Salt of the earth.'

Finn shrank into his chair, aware that he was under scrutiny.

'What's this about your mother?' asked Mrs Cavendish when Mrs Grady had left.

'She died,' said Tara, before Finn could answer. 'Finn is an orphan.'

'Oh dear. I am sorry,' said Mrs Cavendish. 'I had no idea. And your father...?'

'Dead too,' went on Tara.

'Tara!' said her granny. 'Let the boy speak for himself and don't be so insensitive.'

She switched her attention back to Finn, who was now hunched over his stew. He looked up. How do you tell a posh, old-fashioned bird like this that you have no father?

'Mum died last month,' he muttered. 'My father...' he glanced at Tara. She nodded encouragingly. 'My father...' he closed his eyes as he fought for a father. He half smiled at the image that came into his mind. It was just so right. 'My father,' he began again, then cleared his throat. 'He was killed while he was protecting some people. I don't like to talk about it.'

Tara grinned and gave him a discreet thumbs-up. Mrs Cavendish became flustered. Her face softened.

'I'm sorry,' she said again. 'I... I hope you'll be very happy here. What a tragedy.'

Encouraged by her flustering, Finn sat up straight.

'He looked like me,' he said, in a confident voice. 'My father, he looked just like me. He had the very same overbite. See the teeth?' He bared his front teeth, for the first time with pride instead of shame. 'It's a family thing, you understand.'

Tara spluttered and coughed. 'Sorry,' she said, between spasms. 'Crumb went down the wrong way.'

Finn smiled at her. She didn't think I had it in me to invent. I'm not such a wimp. Look at them, they think I'm a brave lad. And I am, Mum. I'm rounding off a family for myself. I'll be the same as anyone else.

'He was a soldier,' he went on. 'High rank.'

'Which army?' asked Mr Cavendish. 'Our family has had its share of military men on both sides of the Irish Sea.'

Tara broke in before Finn could work out that one. 'Shut up, Finn. You know how upset you get if you start on about your father. Let's leave it at that, huh?'

Mr Cavendish and his mother both turned to Tara. Finn could see that they were about to reprimand her. Perhaps he was going a bit too far.

'Tara's right,' he said. 'I'd rather not say any more, if you don't mind.' And then he smiled with a warm, comfortable feeling that had little to do with the hot bread pudding and custard.

Mr Cavendish folded his newspaper and sat back in his chair.

'I have some news,' he said, looking from Mrs Cavendish to Tara. 'Good news. Lots of money.'

'You've won the lottery?' said Tara.

Mr Cavendish shook his head. 'Not quite. I've closed the deal on Cluain na nGall.'

There was an uncomfortable silence.

'It's done, then?' said Mrs Cavendish quietly.

Her son nodded. 'All systems go.'

'What are you talking about?' asked Tara, a shrill note in her voice. 'What about Cluain na nGall?'

'Sold,' said Mr Cavendish. 'Finally offloaded for a tidy sum.'

Tara rose from the table. 'You can't mean it, Dad! What about the family promise never to touch that place. You can't sell it, you just can't. Granny Dob, tell him. This land has been in your family for years and years—'

'Hush, child,' said Mrs Cavendish. 'Your father is right. We can't hold on to a useless field like that. We need the money. Besides, the holiday cottages will brighten the place. There will only be six and they won't intrude on our side of the lake at all.'

'Holiday cottages?' Tara's voice became even more shrill. 'I don't believe it. Crummy tourists in Cluain na nGall? It's... it's a sacred place. The dead Vikings...'

Her father was shaking his head. 'Not a trace of the Vikings. The developer did tests on the soil, put great steel rods down, did soundings. No bones. Or, if there are, they're much too far down to be disturbed by building. The land is quite solid and fit for building on.'

'But there could be artefacts,' went on Tara. 'You can't just plough over artefacts.'

'No artefacts, Tara,' put in Mrs Cavendish. 'The Vikings were buried by Christians at that time. Christians didn't allow any artefacts or armour or weapons to be buried with the dead. And the soundings certainly didn't detect any metal. Anything that's there is, as your father says, very far below the surface. Not worth holding the land for that after all this time. And we really do need the money, dear.'

'You knew about this too?' said Tara. 'Why didn't someone tell me?'

'Because we knew you'd carry on just like you're doing,' replied her father. 'Dob and I discussed this ages ago – it wasn't an easy decision. But it's idle land and not good enough for tillage or grazing. Just think, Tara, you can have fancy clothes, we can have the house done up to its former glory...'

'I don't want fancy clothes,' put in Tara. 'And I like the house just as it is. Can't you change your mind?'

Mr Cavendish shook his head. 'Signed over now,' he said.

'That guy with the shiny shoes you were talking to earlier? Is he the developer?'

Mr Cavendish nodded.

'Well, if I'd known I'd have pushed him into the dung!'

'Tara!' Mrs Cavendish scolded. 'Stop being childish.'

'Fine, I'll go and live with Mum,' said Tara as she flounced from the conservatory.

Finn didn't quite know what to do with himself. He looked awkwardly from granny to father. Mrs Cavendish nodded to him.

'Don't worry,' she said with a smile. 'Tara will come round. She always does. Go and chat to her, there's a good lad.'

Tara was folded in misery on a garden seat, her head resting on her knees. She looked up when Finn approached.

'Traitors, the pair of them,' she muttered. 'That place has always been special. Even now, after we saw those rats, it's still special. Anyway, it was probably all the tests and things that disturbed them.'

Finn sat beside her. 'Well, lucky we got Baldur out when we did. Except that we have to get the hand before they start digging.'

Tara raised her head. 'Huh? Oh, are you still on about your spook. Get real, Finn. This is far more important.'

Finn recoiled. 'You mean you don't believe me?' he cried. 'You still think I've been making it all up?'

Tara put out a hand to stop him getting up. 'I just went along with it,' she said. 'The funeral and all that – it's just a bit of imaginative fun, isn't it? You have a fantastic imagination, Finn. You know you have. That bit about your father was brill—'

But Finn was storming away. All the good things that had been happening were now turning to dust. He was on his own again. Should have known. Why did I have to go telling her all my secrets? Angry, I'm so angry, Mum! It's like I've spread out my soul to be jeered at and trampled on. I hate myself for being such a prat.

He was so angry he didn't notice the small, single pair of glittering eyes that watched him from the bushes on the avenue. Nor did he pay any heed to the traffic hold-up as several wide loads were guided along Main Street.

CHAPTER FIFTEEN

'Had you a nice time?' Meg looked up from the ironing when Finn came into the kitchen. 'I didn't know you'd made friends with the Cavendish girl. Goodness, aren't we going up in the world?'

Finn said nothing. He looked down at the bottom of the back door and saw that Bill had nailed on another piece of wood. Meg noticed his interest.

'That was some night, wasn't it?' she went on. 'That environmental health man wasn't much use to us, was he? Didn't believe us, the old troutface.' She shook out a pillow cover and spread it on the ironing board. 'Bill says that there's only a chance in a million of that happening, that something must have disturbed them. He says they won't come back, but I've made him fix that gap just in case. What do you think, Finn?'

Does it really matter what I think? Those rats were after Baldur, but how can I tell her that? She'd dismiss it, say things were playing tricks on my mind, just like Tara.

He shrugged. 'Don't know.'

Meg sighed as she continued with the ironing. Finn knew she was finding it hard going, trying to get words out of him. But that was her problem. He hadn't asked to come here.

'Just as well to be sure, though,' he muttered.

Meg smiled, relieved that he had at least made some response. She folded the pillow cover and ran the iron over it again so that there would be neat lines on it.

'So, was the dinner nice?' she asked.

'It was all right,' said Finn. Questions. Here we go again.

'Nice house? I've never been. I've only ever seen it from the lake. It's big, isn't it?'

'It's OK,' said Finn. 'I think I'll just go out, get some air.'

He took a breath as he closed the back door behind him. Stifled, that's how I feel. Smothered in questions. It's like people want to get inside your head and dig out your thoughts so that they can jump on them. Told you though, Mum, didn't I? Told you my thoughts. But you went away and took all my thoughts with you.

Bill looked up when he saw the boy run past him, climb over the gate to the meadow, and continue running as if to escape pursuing demons.

'Hello, Finn,' he called out.

But Finn just kept running. Bill shook his head and made his way to the kitchen. Meg was folding the ironing board.

'Where's that boy off to?' he asked. 'Galloped past without so much as a word.'

Meg shook her head sadly. 'It's not going terribly well, is it, Bill? she said sadly. 'I was beginning to think we might be getting through to him, but,' she shrugged, 'we're back to where we started. I tried to make conversation about his dinner. I was thrilled he'd made a friend. Maybe that's the problem.'

'What do you mean?' Bill looked up from pulling off his wellingtons.

Meg began putting the folded clothes into the airing cupboard beside the range.

'We're not good enough,' she muttered. 'He's ashamed of us. We're older and we're just a plain pair, you and me.'

'Rubbish, woman,' retorted Bill. 'He's just a confused young fellow. Probably still scared after last night's skirmish. Give him time.'

'Bet he wasn't a confused young fellow at dinner up there in the big house,' said Meg, with a touch of bitterness. 'Bet there was no shortage of talk with them. No, I'm telling you, Bill Griffith, we're not grand enough for him.'

'Well, if we're not, then that's his tough luck,' said Bill. 'You were good enough to take him on, even though you hadn't seen his mother for years. It's up to him to make this work, we can't do any more. Just bide our time.'

Meg sighed as she closed the door of the airing cupboard.

'Proud, I suppose. Just like Ann. She wouldn't accept help from any of us. Went off to the city to bring up Finn on her own. Now here we are stuck with a stranger, and he with us.'

'She was young,' said Bill gently. 'Her parents being killed in that car accident when she was twenty didn't help. The lad was all she had, Meg. She probably wanted a new beginning for herself and her son. Like I said, give him time.'

Meg wrapped the flex around the handle of the iron and stood it at the back of the kitchen unit.

'What choice have we?' she said. 'You know, he hasn't even unpacked yet. It's like he's poised for flight. What do we do if he decides to run away?'

'There you go, imagining things,' laughed Bill. 'Come on, I'll make you a cup of tea. Things will work out.'

Finn didn't stop running until he'd gone beyond the meadow to the stretch of trees that marked the boundary of Bill and Meg's land. There was an overgrown path through the trees. Finn kept going, galloping through the nettles and high grass until, with a gasp of surprise, he found himself at the lakeshore. He flung himself down, breathless, and looked at the surrounding landscape. For as far as he could see, in that whole panorama, he was the only person.

And that was how it was going to be. Never again would he let anyone break through his defences. Nobody would hurt him ever again. He stood up and went closer to the reeds that grew in abundance around the edge of the lake. It was then he saw the small dilapidated mooring almost hidden from sight. Further up, away from the water, was an upturned boat, its oars neatly lined up beside it. Another time he would have been delighted by this discovery, but right now there was too much on his mind. Especially when he saw, away over on the other side of the lake, the roof and chimneys of Tara's house peeping up over the trees. He brushed aside the image of Tara's laughing face. He didn't want to know. She'd let him down, and that was what mattered. And she'd let Baldur down, dismissed him as a concoction of Finn's imagination. How could she pretend that she even partly believed him and then make him out to be a fool? In anger he threw a stick at a clump of nettles. Something stirred, something that he'd disturbed.

Finn jumped back when he saw the rat. Breathless as he was, he turned and fled, panic making his heart thump at a rate of knots. They weren't going to let up, were they? Baldur! The awful dread of what he had to do filled his mind like a black cloud as he ran. The hand that was still buried, the unfinished raft, Baldur's funeral – how could he ever get all that sorted by midnight tomorrow night? Especially now, with the rats still shadowing him. He sobbed with fear as he ran. He slammed the back door after him and leaned against it, panting and sobbing at the same time.

Fibbing that he had a headache, he went to bed early. Meg had fussed, of course, bringing him hot milk. But sleep was slow in coming. He could hear the murmur of voices from the kitchen. Him. It had to be him they were talking about because he'd practically screeched at them to lock everywhere. Bill had tried to calm him, told him it was a one-off thing, the rat episode. But when Finn had persisted, he'd agreed to double-check everywhere. Now they were locking up. He could hear them rattling the window catches. Rats! Guilt. If it wasn't for me they wouldn't have to go through this. Their own fault. They shouldn't have dragged me here. But deep down, in some closed-off chamber of his mind was the niggling thought that they hadn't actually dragged him here. He'd come because there was no place else to go. Not to worry, he thought as he turned over and tried to coax some sleep, when he'd looked after Baldur he'd leave this place. And leave fickle Tara. Some friend she'd turned out to be. Still, it was her laughing face that was in his mind when sleep did come.

It was the cold that woke Finn. He glanced fearfully at the window, but he knew he'd locked it securely. No rats. He shivered and pulled the duvet around his shoulders.

'I'm greatly afraid,' said the deep whispering voice of Baldur.

Finn shot up straight. 'What?' he said, peering at the tall figure at the end of the bed. He was overcome with a terrible dread, not of the familiar figure of Baldur, but for Baldur's safety. Had the rats found their way to the skull?

'Is it your head?' he asked.

'No,' replied Baldur. 'It's my hand, boy.'

'Your hand? Have the rats—?'

'No, not the rats. The machines. They have moved in the great machines to start work tomorrow morning. You must get my hand before they cover it. All will be lost if you don't put my hand with my head.'

'I was going to do that in the morning,' said Finn.

Baldur leaned closer. 'That might be too late,' he said. 'By the time you find it, the men will have come to dig the land. Can you come now?'

'Now?' Finn looked at the luminous hands of the Humpty Dumpty clock that he'd put together again and propped up on his bedside table because his watch had stopped. 'It's half-past four, Baldur. Surely it would be OK to go there at seven? It'll be daylight then.'

Baldur sat on the edge of the bed and looked pleadingly at Finn. 'Perhaps you think I fuss too much, boy.'

'Finn,' put in Finn. 'I have a name too, you know.'

Baldur nodded. 'Finn,' he said, his overbite emphasising the f. 'This is my last chance at happiness. If I don't have my funeral ritual, then I lose Áine for ever.'

'I know,' said Finn. 'You told me. I'm doing it. Haven't you seen the raft?'

Baldur held up his hand. 'But as well as that,' he went on, 'with the thousand year time limit over, the spirit of Lua will rule this place. His evil will take over the land surrounding the burial site. The people who allow the land to be ploughed up will be cursed. They will be haunted and they will die.'

'Tara!' exclaimed Finn. 'Tara and her family!'

'They will die,' repeated Baldur. 'One by one, from disease or accident. The only thing that can prevent that is my ritual funeral. That will break Lua's power.'

'Oh no,' groaned Finn. 'Things are getting worse. I don't think I can go through with this, Baldur.'

Baldur reached out and touched Finn's arm. Finn's instinct to pull away stopped when, to his amazement, he realised the touch was warm and comforting.

'Don't stop now, Finn,' said Baldur. 'I'm depending on you. You're my only hope. You're also the only hope of the people you speak of. Their lives and my spirit's freedom to be united with my lady.'

Finn groaned again. Could his life be any bleaker than it was right now?

'I can remain with you until daybreak,' said Baldur.

Reluctantly Finn pulled on his jeans and trainers. Together the boy and his spectral companion eased their way down the stairs.

'No rats,' whispered Baldur when he saw Finn look warily through the kitchen window. 'Not here. Not now that you've moved my head.'

'They were at the lake,' Finn replied. 'This evening I saw some at the lake. Well, just one, but I'm sure there were more. At least it felt like that.'

Baldur shrugged. 'Scouts,' he said. 'Just watching you to see where you are. They will watch until...' he stopped.

'Until?' prompted Finn.

'Until it is time.'

'Time for what? Stop speaking in half-riddles, Baldur.'

'Time for my ritual funeral,' went on Baldur. 'They will watch until then.'

'And then? Come on, don't stop. I can't get much more terrified than I am now.'

'Please,' said Baldur. 'Let us just take one step at a time.'

Finn nodded. Maybe it was better not to know what could lie ahead, he might just go back to bed and turn into a gibbering nutcase. And then Meg and Bill would really regret taking him on. Bill! That reminded him! Just before he opened the back door, Finn pulled a chair over to the dresser.

'Hang on a sec, Baldur,' he whispered. 'I've got to get something here. Something for the rats.'

CHAPTER SIXTEEN

Finn felt exposed and vulnerable. He glanced around nervously as he walked with the ghost. But it's different this time. I have Baldur to protect me. That's even better than having an ordinary person to share this with me. Baldur was – is – a powerful warrior. He'll watch out for me. Baldur won't let any harm come to me.

'What have you been doing all this time?' asked Finn, as they took the route up the hill to the spot where Finn had first met Tara. 'For the past thousand years, what were you doing?'

'Waiting patiently for someone like you to come along. Someone I knew I could trust.'

'Someone who just happened to pull your head out of a hole in the ground,' put in Finn.

'Fate,' said Baldur. 'A preordained meeting. It was right that it should be you, Finn.'

'Thanks a whole bunch,' muttered Finn. 'I could have done without all this hassle.'

Baldur stopped and looked at him with a mixture of

sadness and surprise. 'You're sorry I've come into your life?' he said.

Finn frowned. Then he shook his head. 'Funny that. I'm really quite glad that I've got to know you. I think it's the teeth.'

'Teeth?' said Baldur.

'Like mine. I look at you and I feel sort of – I know it's weird – but I feel we're mates. Mates with over a thousand years between us. And you don't scare me. I never thought I'd be chatting to a spook, never mind putting my neck in a noose to do one favours.'

'I didn't set out to scare you,' said Baldur. 'If I had wanted to scare you, you would be gibbering incoherently with fright by now. No, I knew you were the one when you first picked up my head. It was a comfortable feeling.'

'That's it!' said Finn. 'Comfortable. What a pity I couldn't have been with you way back then, or that you couldn't stay with me, now.'

'Well, whatever time we have left together, Finn,' said Baldur, 'it is good that we are friends.'

The trees were silhouetted against the navy blue of the pre-dawn sky. A pigeon cooed softly. Other than that, there was a silence. Nothing stirred. At least nothing above ground stirred.

'Was it awful?' whispered Finn.

'Was what awful?'

'The battle. Was it awful?'

Baldur said nothing for a few moments. Then he gave a great sigh.

'It was horrendous,' he said. 'These fields,' he stopped and gestured all around, 'were splashed red with the blood of men from both sides. I had been in battles before, when I was a Viking raider. At that time we used to attack monasteries, take their treasure back to Norway. We didn't meet with much resistance. The monasteries were peopled by religious men who led peaceful lives.'

'Did you kill?' asked Finn.

Baldur made an apologetic grimace. 'That's how it was then,' he said. 'But then I came to like this place and decided to stay. You know the rest.'

'And the battle?' said Finn. They were now passing through the grove of trees. Ahead they could see the grotesque silhouettes of the diggers, poised for work in the morning.

'This was not like taking a monastery,' replied Baldur. 'This was a battle between strong, highly trained warriors pitted against one another in hand-to-hand fighting. The most frightening sound was the screaming. I can hear them still, the screams of battle – anger mixed with the screams of pain. Try to imagine the face of someone running towards you wielding an axe, with a hatred born of battle. And you know either you or he will die, so you become twisted with hatred too. You scream and he screams. But then, of course, I died and didn't hear the screams any more.'

Finn was on the point of asking Baldur what it was like to die, but the shadowy, slithering forms that were emerging from the Viking burial ground turned the words into a gasp of horror.

'Rats!' he whispered to Baldur. 'It's the rats.'

'I expected that,' said Baldur. 'They don't want you to get my hand. Curses on them!'

'Can't you do anything?' asked Finn in desperation as the forms moved silently towards them.

'I'm afraid not,' said Baldur. 'Until I have my hero's funeral, I have no power to stop them. I'm sorry.'

'Oh jeez, Baldur!' Finn wailed. 'I thought I was safe with you. If I'd known—'

'Just do what you can. Be brave. You can do it, Finn. Calm and determined, just like in battle.'

With a grunt, Finn took the cartridges he'd stuffed into his pocket and slotted one into Bill's shotgun. He swallowed hard, lifted the gun to his shoulder and aimed at the moving mass. He shut his eyes as he pulled the trigger. His own scream blended with the screams of the rats as the gun kicked back on his shoulder.

'More screams!' cried Baldur. 'One thousand years later we have more screams.'

'So would you be screaming if you got a whack from a shotgun,' said Finn, nursing his shoulder and at the same time trying to load up again. He could see the rats re-forming.

'A "whack" as you call it, whether from a shotgun or a battleaxe is certainly something to make even the bravest scream,' said Baldur. 'But a warrior must never lose concentration on the enemy. Watch, Finn. Watch the rats. Our enemies.'

'Come on, scum,' Finn shouted down his fear as he aimed again. This time he was ready for the kickback. Once more the rats scattered and once more Finn loaded the shotgun. 'I don't know how long I can hold them off,' he cried.

'Until daybreak,' said Baldur. 'If you can just keep them away from you until daybreak, then you will be safe.'

'What happens if I don't keep them off?' said Finn as he loaded up again. Baldur didn't reply. Finn looked at him before aiming again. 'Baldur? What happens—?'

'Concentrate, lad,' Baldur said with a touch of panic in his ghostly voice.

Finn swallowed again. 'They'd kill me, wouldn't they? They'd kill me rather than let me get the hand for your funeral, isn't that right?'

'Yes,' muttered Baldur.

'Oh God!' breathed Finn. 'And if I turn and run like blazes?'

'They would follow.'

'So,' Finn grunted as he loaded up again, 'I'm stuck here with a few cartridges and a useless spook who can't help me? Blast you to hell, rats!' he roared as he pulled the trigger again. His arms were getting tired. Maybe he should just lie down and die. Then he and Baldur could mooch about eternity together. Two goofy spooks. His laughter was hysterical as he blasted yet again. And still they came. The cartridges were dwindling. Finn remembered a film he'd watched with Mum. A cowboy film where someone had said, 'Don't shoot until you see the whites of their eyes'. Do rats have whites in their eyes? He wasn't going to wait to find out. Blam! Another blast. But the slithering flood was almost on him. One cartridge left. He was panting as he slotted it in. Aim. Blam! That was it. Finn shut his eyes again, waited for the first bite.

'This is it, Baldur,' he cried. 'Sorry about your—'

Barking? Rats don't bark! Finn's eyes shot open.

'Baldur?'

But Baldur had gone. And so had the rats – both dead and living. The sun was just visible as an orange crescent above the trees. Finn sank to the ground and sobbed again, this time with relief. He'd beaten them. He'd beaten the rats. Now all he had to do was get the hand. The barking broke in on his thoughts again. It was coming from beyond the trees. The urge to flee took over every nerve in Finn's body. But before he could do so, Tara's father and Stanley appeared in the gloom. Finn froze. Flight was out of the question now. He'd been seen. Besides, those snarling Rottweilers wouldn't let him get very far. His body went limp and he stood, waiting for the men and the dogs to come closer.

CHAPTER SEVENTEEN

Click, click.

'Humpty bloody Dumpty', Finn swore softly. He should have left him where he had fallen, with his stupid grin and his constant click click reminding Finn that the day was passing. He was in disgrace. There had been a terrible scene, made all the worse because he couldn't explain what he was really doing on the site at five o'clock in the morning with a shotgun. Helping a spook? That a curse would befall the Cavendish family? Who'd believe a story like that? He'd been hauled back to the house with threats of being charged with trespass with an offensive weapon.

'Shooting rats indeed,' said Mr Cavendish, taking the gun from Finn. 'You expect me to believe that?'

'It's true,' Finn replied in a very small voice as he slumped along between the two men and the leash-straining watchdogs. But, just like the episode with the health officer, there was not even one body of a rat to prove his point. Stanley went to ring the police when they got to the kitchen, but by then Mr Cavendish had cooled down a bit.

'No,' he said. 'I'll just call the lad's folks. Let them decide what to do.'

And so Bill had come to collect Finn. Finn couldn't bear to remember the look of hurt and shame on Bill's face. Bill had tried to explain to Mr Cavendish that Finn had a consuming fear of rats since the freak incident the night before. But Mr Cavendish was dismissive.

'Take him home,' he said. 'I won't press charges this time. Just don't come around here any more, Finn.'

At least Finn didn't have to suffer the indignity of Tara or her granny being present.

Bill hadn't said anything much on the way home. In fact Finn would have preferred it if he'd exploded with anger. The hurt silence was almost more than he could endure.

'I'm sorry,' Finn said when they pulled up in front of the house. 'It was the rats.'

'OK, lad,' said Bill, with just a slight hint of impatience. 'Let's forget about the rats, eh? I know you were scared last night – we all were. But let's not get one freak occurrence way out of proportion. Best go to your room now. I'll explain to Meg.'

Finn hesitated at the foot of the stairs. He could hear Meg in the kitchen, no doubt anxiously awaiting an explanation. He turned to say something to Bill – anything to wipe the hurt from the old man's face. But Bill nodded in a kindly way.

'Go on now,' he said. 'We'll talk later.'

And now it was later. Much later. Meg had insisted on giving him a sleeping pill, said things would seem better after a good sleep. Finn had been so remorseful that he hadn't had the heart to refuse her kind gesture. And now, here he was muzzy-headed and out of time. Finn turned towards the clicking Humpty Dumpty again. Why does time gallop when you want it to crawl? I've let everyone down, Mum. Baldur, Meg, Bill, Tara and her family – I've failed them all. And I've lost. Everything is lost now. He sat on the side of the bed, his elbows resting on the window ledge. Away out there, beyond the meadow and the trees stood Tara's house. Finn groaned and buried his head in his arms. Tara was probably over there hating him for being such a touchy grouch with a chip on his shoulder. If he could just rub out that moment when they'd parted on bad terms and start again, he'd never be a grouch ever again. What should he do? Ring and tell her about the awful curse that was about to fall on her family because he'd failed to keep his promise to Baldur? That would really cause her to consider him a nutcase. Besides, it would probably be the nosy granny who'd answer and he'd just become a gibbering nerd. He made a fist with one hand and punched the other in a gesture of helpless frustration.

But hang on, the day wasn't over yet! Am I going to stay sitting here feeling sorry for myself? Pull yourself together, Finn. Things to do. Finn swung around and looked at the clock again, suddenly alert. Eight o'clock. He had four hours to make one last attempt. But how to do it? He was banned from the Cavendish estate and from any contact with Tara. How could he get to the raft and finish it? And Baldur's skull – how could he get to the shed without being seen going through the orchard? He pushed his thumb under his front teeth and swayed back and forth on the bed. He looked out again at the peaceful scene that only he knew was laden with foreboding. Lonely, desperate feeling.

And then it hit him. The lake! Out there, beyond the trees was the lake that skirted Tara's place! If that old boat he'd seen yesterday was watertight, he could sail around the lake and moor beside the old shed. Tara had said nobody ever went there. Surely Mrs Cavendish wouldn't wander down that far in the late evening. He'd just have to take a chance on that. His heart pounded with anticipation.

Downstairs was quiet. He paused on the landing to listen. Nothing stirring. He took a deep breath and ventured further down the stairs. He froze when a step creaked. He waited for the kitchen door to open. No response. He got to the front door and quietly let himself out. Then he realised he couldn't close it without slamming it, so he left it slightly ajar. They'd miss him, he knew that. Should have rolled up some clothes and put them under the duvet to look like he was still asleep. Nothing he could do now. He could explain later, right now the most important task of his life had to be tackled. Trying not to think negative thoughts. Would there be rats? Would the boat be full of holes? Would he get to the raft undetected? – he ran once more through the meadow. And the hand? He expelled a breath. What about the hand? First things first. When the raft was finished he'd have to try and get the hand. Would it be already buried? Would there be a watchman on the site? So many obstacles. Maybe it would be better to turn back. Yeah, Finn. Spend the rest of your life with an even bigger chip on your shoulder because you didn't try. Get on with it! With renewed determination, he ran even faster.

The boat looked sound enough. He turned it over, put in the oars and dragged it to the water's edge. So far so good, he thought, as it bobbed up and down on the ripples. With a fearful look behind to see if there were any rats following, Finn pushed away from the reeds. The rusty rowlocks creaked when he inserted the oars, but they moved with the oars and he soon got the knack of rowing. He kept to the edge of the lake, easing the boat through the reeds. The sun was turning into its evening scarlet. Finn wished with all his heart that he'd spat out the sleeping pill. He should have held it under his tongue and spat it out when Meg left the room. But he'd wanted to please her, wipe the puzzled pain from her face, so he'd swallowed the pill. And now he'd lost precious hours. He sweated as he urged the boat to go faster. Now and then he jumped as he disturbed a water hen, but at least there were no rats. Not yet. He knew they were watching, somewhere they were poised. And he didn't even have a gun this time.

Around by the trees now, not far to go. And there it was, the mooring beside the old shed. Holding his breath, Finn pulled in and tied up the boat. Then he crept towards the shed, hid behind some bushes, and peered all around. All quiet. OK, courage, let's make a start.

The raft was exactly as he and Tara had left it yesterday. Only yesterday? It seemed more like years. The blue and red buoys they'd found in the boathouse were ready for lashing on. Finn set to. The long shadow from the shed made him shiver with the sudden drop in temperature of shade after sun. He grunted with effort as he wound the ropes around the buoys and got them under the crisscross laths. Now the sun was poised low over the lake. Not much daylight left. Apart from finding it difficult to work in the gloom of a summer twilight, Finn was filled with dread at what terrors the night would bring. He quickened his pace, had to get this finished. Now and then he glanced warily around for glittering eyes or the all-too familiar flow of rat bodies. He almost freaked out into a blubbering mess when a voice said:

'Want a hand?'

CHAPTER EIGHTEEN

'Tara!' Finn exclaimed, when he'd had time to catch his breath. 'What are you doing here?'

'What do you think I'm doing, silly?' she said, her fingers tucked into the straps of a small rucksack she was carrying on her back. 'I've come to help. Didn't I say I would? I knew you'd be back. I knew you'd be too... too stubbornly honourable to let down your spook. I've been watching out for you all day. What kept you till now? I was beginning to think the worst, that you'd been flung in the nick or else sent back to wherever you came from.'

'I was asleep,' Finn said sheepishly.

'Asleep!' Tara put her hands on her hips and looked at him with dismay. 'Lazy git. And there was me chewing my toenails with worry about you. How could you sleep?'

'Sshh,' said Finn, 'It's a long story.'

'Oh I know the story,' laughed Tara. 'I heard all about your weird shooting spree in the wee small hours. Dad is not pleased to think that someone he'd shared a dinner with would come back with a shotgun. He thinks you were out to damage the machinery because of me.'

'Huh?'

'That time I went off in a huff because of the land being sold to a property developer, Dad thinks you came back to try and knock the machinery out of commission to please me.'

'As if,' said Finn softly. 'And what did you tell him?'

'Oh, I told him you were harmless. Screw loose, but entirely harmless.'

'Thanks very much, I don't think,' muttered Finn.

Tara laughed again. In spite of the situation, Finn laughed with her. It was good to hear her voice again. The weight of dread lifted a bit. He wasn't alone, but there was still much to be done and so much to fear. He looked at Tara as she began to lash more buoys to the laths of wood. Should he tell her all he knew? That the lives of herself and her family depended on what they were doing? No, better not. He might really lose her if he did. How could she not think him crazy if he came out with a statement like that? He took a deep breath and got back to the work of finishing the raft.

'Don't you want to know what happened?' Finn asked eventually.

Tara held up her hand. 'If it's more spooky stuff, then no thanks. I just know that there's some black shadow inside your head that won't go away until you've done this. One of those mental blokes – you know, Freud and his lot – would probably make something of it. But I think that when you've done this, you have a fair chance of being normal again.'

Finn stopped what he was doing and looked at her, mouth open.

'You think I'm a nutcase?'

'Yeah, sure. But I have nothing against nutcases. My family is full of them. Take Granny Dob—'

'No thanks,' said Finn, glad to get in a riposte of his own. 'I'd rather not.'

More tinkling laughter. 'Touché! Enough talk, let's get this show on the road – or on the lake rather. And,' she added excitedly, 'I have a mega surprise—'

The rustle in the bushes caused them both to freeze.

'Your granny?' whispered Finn.

Tara shook her head. 'Gone to bridge.'

The bushes rustled again. 'Nor my dad,' went on Tara. 'He's gone to see Mum and won't be back for two days.'

Finn wished it was Tara's dad because, when he saw the grey shapes moving in the undergrowth, he knew that now was the time for the worst of terror.

'The raft!' he exclaimed. 'Help me get it into the shed. Quickly!'

Tara was puzzled. 'What?' she began, but Finn shouted her down.

'Grab the other end of the raft, Tara! We've got to get it into the shed. They'll wreck it.'

'Who? What are you on about, Finn?'

'Just do it!'

'Don't tell me—'

'Tara, trust me! Move!'

His voice frightened Tara. The extreme urgency of his tone made her comply. She took one end of the raft and tried to keep up with Finn as he charged towards the shed carrying the other end. When they got inside, he set about barricading the door with anything that came to hand. She was trapped in a shed, in the gloom of twilight, with a total madman.

'Finn,' Tara began in a tremulous voice. 'I'm dead scared. Please let me go home. I won't say anything, honest.'

Finn was standing to one side of the window. 'Here they come,' he said.

Tara screamed when the rats hit the window. Slap, slap, slap. One by one they smacked against it, white bellies pressed against the glass. She screamed again when she heard them scrabbling at the bottom of the door. But when Baldur emerged from the shadows, she fell to the floor like a rag doll.

'Tara,' Finn was patting her face. 'Come on, Tara. You're a tough cookie, don't pass out on us.'

On us? Tara opened her eyes. Finn's white, anxious face was peering at her. But, over his shoulder another face was peering at her too. A grey face that looked like an older, ghostly version of Finn.

'Baldur?' she whispered, pushing herself back along the stone floor.

'Don't be scared,' said Finn. 'This is my good friend Baldur. He's the one we're going to give the ritual funeral. At least we hope to give the ritual funeral,' he went on, standing up and looking at the rat-crowded window. 'It's not looking good, is it, Baldur?'

Baldur gave a ghostly sigh and shook his head sadly. The scrabbling and squealing from outside the shed was escalating. Tara got to her feet and stood like someone in a trance. She stared at Baldur, unsure which to be more scared of – his ghostly figure or the menacing rats.

'Put more stuff against the door,' Finn's voice startled her into action. 'They mustn't get in. We'll lose everything if they do.' Mainly our lives and Baldur's freedom, he thought.

The summer twilight was beginning to cast a deeper gloom as Finn and Tara dragged everything they could lay their hands on to the door.

'It just takes one,' panted Finn. 'It just takes one of those slimeballs to get through and it's all over.'

'Please tell me I'm dreaming,' said Tara, finding her voice at last.

'Wish you were,' said Finn, grunting with effort as he shouldered an old cupboard against the barricade.

When there was nothing left to add, the two youngsters drew back, exhausted. Tara flopped into one of the chairs they'd dusted off for their cosy hideaway – was it yesterday or a hundred years ago? So much had happened. Finn stayed near the door, watching, waiting.

'What now, Baldur?' he asked. 'How are we to get the raft to the lake?'

Baldur sank into the other chair. 'Oh, I'm weary,' he said. 'One thousand years I've waited for this and now...' he gestured towards the rats that were still piling up on the window. 'Now it would seem that all is lost.'

Finn moved away from the barricade and stood before his ghostly friend.

'After all that,' he muttered despondently. 'All we did. All for nothing. After blasting those sneaky rats off in the early hours of this morning. And now, just when we were ready to carry out the funeral, they have us trapped.' He took a deep breath to hold down the panic that was rising in his chest.

Baldur reached out towards Finn. 'You've done all you could, lad,' he said. 'You can't fight evil. It defeated me one thousand years ago and, even though it may defeat me now, I must make my stand against the might of Lua. The rats will follow me. Then you and the girl can go home.'

Tara looked at Finn's pained face and, in that fleeting moment, saw that every fantasy that Finn had ever had was wrapped up in that goofy ghost. She jumped up.

'Hang on a sec here,' she said, the old Tara back in action. 'You two sound like a couple of wimps.'

The boy and the ghost turned to look at her.

'Listen to yourselves,' she went on. 'OK, so there's a bunch of rats outside. We can get past them – they're only vermin.'

'No, Tara,' said Finn. 'They're not just ordinary rats. Even their dead bodies disappear as if they melt into the ground.'

'Netherworld rats,' explained Baldur. 'They are under the evil power of Lua. He's the man who killed me. Those rats have been groomed to kill rather than let me have my hero's funeral.'

Tara turned this over in her mind for a moment as the three of them listened to the rat sounds reaching towards a crescendo.

'OK,' she said. 'So we either stay in here wetting our pants with fear, waiting for that lot to get through, or we bloomin' well get our act together and at least give them something to think about, the scum. I'm certainly not going to cower here.'

Finn and Baldur looked at one another.

'She's right, Baldur,' said Finn. 'You were a great hero once, you can't let go without a fight. I don't know what we'll do, but we'll go down fighting.' Baldur suddenly stood up straight, his shoulders thrown back and his head held high.

'Yes,' he said, in a strong voice. 'I was a great hero and I'm still a great hero. The evil Lua won't beat Baldur, Master of Arms to Chieftain O'Brien.'

'That's it, old pal,' said Finn, suddenly realising that now it was a case of either gathering every shred of courage and strength or else going under as a gibbering loser. 'This time you've got Tara and me.'

Strangely enough, he hadn't felt so alive for a long

time. Perhaps it had to do with having an immediate and urgent purpose to his life that made everything shoot into perspective. Or maybe you feel extra alive just before your life is taken away. Is that how it is, Mum?

The three of them looked at the window, the writhing mass still pressing against the glass, almost blocking out what was left of the dusk.

'That glass won't hold,' said Baldur, his heroic pose slipping.

'A few boards,' said Finn. 'And pull those heavy curtains across. There are nails, but we'll have to look for boards. If we can find any in this light.'

'Ha,' said Tara. 'We have light. I brought down candles this morning – remember, Finn, – I said I would? Thought you might be here, in spite of your shenanigans in the wee small hours. But no, you were asleep for the day, weren't you?'

'I told you,' Finn muttered, looking at Baldur to see how he was taking that bit of useless information. 'Meg made me take a sl—'

'Oh, just kidding,' said Tara. 'Look, here are the candles. Loads of them. Matches too. Light some. There's no time to lose.'

Baldur stayed in the shadows while Tara went about placing the candles around the shed, some on the candelabra, the rest in discarded bottles. Finn broke up bits of wood and began to hammer them into the window frame. The sharp teeth, twitching whiskers and white bellies were close to his face, but there was no time to let fear take hold.

'Any chance of some light here?' he called to Tara.

She stood on a box and raised a candle to where Finn had begun hammering. As soon as it lit up the window, the rats disappeared with echoing screeches.

'Jeez! Did you see that?' exclaimed Finn, hammer poised. 'Gone in a split second. It's the light,' he added gleefully.

'That is true,' put in Baldur. 'They are afraid of the light. Quickly, put some candles around the window.'

Tara and Finn stuck more candles into anything that would hold them and arranged them along the window ledge. Then they pulled away the curtains so that they wouldn't catch fire.

'Sshh,' whispered Tara as they climbed down. 'Listen.'

'The scratching at the door has stopped,' said Finn. 'We've beaten them, the toerags.'

'They are patient,' said Baldur, from the shadows. 'They are dangerously patient. They have waited and watched for one thousand years. They will wait.'

'Maybe not,' said Finn, more in doubt than in hope. 'Maybe we can keep fires going, make some sort of a flaming torch to keep them back while we run to the lake – if they stay around. That's it – we'll make some flaming torches and light them at the last minute. What time is it?' he went on, looking at his watch, forgetting the batteries were dead.

Tara held her wrist towards the candlelight. 'Three minutes past eleven,' she said.

Finn shut his eyes and groaned. 'Less than an hour,' he whispered.

Tara nodded. Baldur grimaced.

'Useless,' he groaned. 'I feel so useless. You are doing this for me and I cannot help. Let it go. Let them have me. There's nothing to be gained from prolonging—'

'Oh, do shut up, you daft spook!' exclaimed Tara. 'We'll fight them.'

'But you, girl,' went on Baldur. 'You are in danger too! You and your—' He broke off when Finn frowned at him and shook his head. There was enough going on without driving feisty Tara into a panic. Baldur looked helpless as he sank back into the shadows.

'There's no point in just standing there,' continued Finn, striding purposefully over to Baldur and thrusting his determined face close to the ghost. 'We're all in danger. Tara's right, we can't stop now. Come on, Baldur, get that old heroism on course again. Think of all the battles you've fought and won. Let's get the raft ready. At least we'll have that much done. Come on, up off your ghostly behind. You're going to make this work. We can't do this without you.'

Outside, the rats were huddled into a silent mass. Expectant, waiting. The Master would come soon. They poised themselves, waiting for his word. Soon it would be time.

While Finn pulled the raft into the middle of the floor, Tara bent down and listened at the door.

'Not a sound,' she whispered. 'They've definitely gone. The light has done the trick. There's something I don't understand though,' she went on. 'If they're afraid of the light, how come we saw them in daylight the other day? And tonight – it wasn't quite dark when they came.'

Baldur nodded. 'Scouts,' he said. 'It was scouts you saw. The light doesn't affect them. It's the rats from deep down that are dangerous. The scouts were simply charged with following my bones should they ever be moved.'

'As they were,' put in Tara, jerking her head towards Finn.

'Just so,' said Baldur. 'And then it was their duty to send word to the underground guardians where to come, and to take the bones back. So, here we are, regretfully, in a shed towards midnight not knowing what's outside. I feel so sorry.'

'Stop sinking into that stupid talk,' Finn said angrily. 'You can do it. You can beat this creep, I know you can. And there are no regrets – certainly none from me. I'm glad I took your head.'

Baldur blinked. Then, once more he drew himself up. Bravery that had lain dormant for a thousand years needed quite a prodding. Finn's determined words and confidence in him was making him feel stronger.

'So, let's get on with that raft, then,' said Tara. 'Let's take one thing at a time and do it right. Don't think about out there. Concentrate on what we can do right now.'

Finn nodded approvingly at her. 'Too right,' he said. 'So,what do we need, Baldur? Besides your head and—' he broke off and slapped his forehead. 'The hand! I clean forgot about the hand! Tara! Where are you going? Don't try to go out in case—'

But Tara had stopped where she had left the small rucksack she'd had on her back and was rummaging in it. 'Here we are,' she said, holding something up.

'A bunch of twigs!' exclaimed Finn. 'What good is that?'

'Excuse me, that is my hand you're talking about,' put in Baldur. 'That hand has won battles, I'll have you know, young man.'

Tara was grinning. 'That time I asked you if you wanted a hand, Finn, I really meant it, see? This is the mega surprise I'd started to tell you about. I figured when I heard about your disgrace that you probably didn't get what you were looking for, so I went to the Viking plot after breakfast and sifted around.'

'You're ace,' said Finn, with amazement. 'I can't believe you did that. In spite of the rats and in spite of thinking I was talking garbage, you went and did this?'

Tara shrugged modestly. 'I'd nothing better to do. Anyway I timed it so that the workmen would be there. They tried to run me, but I put on my daughter-of-the-manor-house act and even got one of them to hang around near me while I looked for the bracelet

159

I pretended I'd lost. It was just a matter of sweeping the hand into my bag before he saw it. Simple really.'

'No it wasn't simple,' said Finn. 'You were scared of the rats, I bet.'

'Yes,' agreed Tara. 'But I had a macho guy on standby, didn't I? He even lent me his big industrial gloves so that my delicate handies wouldn't get dirty.'

'Thank you, lady,' said Baldur, giving an old-fashioned bow. 'That took a lot of courage. I wished I could have helped.'

'You knew?' said Finn, turning to the ghost.

Baldur nodded. 'Certainly. I was watching. I've been watching my bones for a thousand years, remember. And that's why Tara can see me now. Only people who have my bones can see me.'

A candle spluttered, reminding the trio that time was ticking away.

'OK, what do we need?' Finn asked again.

Baldur stood over the raft and looked at it thoughtfully, shading his eyes from the light.

'Apart from my bones,' he began, 'there should be a weapon.'

'Check!' said Finn, suddenly catching sight of the lance. 'Will that do?' he fetched it and held it out to Baldur.

Baldur smiled. 'Admirably,' he said, running his spectral hand along the shaft, just as Finn had done. 'Then there's my death rune.'

'Your what?' Finn and Tara said together.

'Rune,' Baldur said again. 'It's a stone with Viking symbols on it.'

'Oh, come on, Baldur,' groaned Finn. 'We wouldn't have a clue.'

'Perhaps I could do it myself,' said Baldur. 'See? My body is getting stronger.'

And so it was. From being a ghostly grey, he was becoming more solid. His long, untidy hair shone flaxen in the candlelight. His high cheekbones and bearded chin made him look more like a brave warrior than a limp ghost. What had been a ragged shroud had now turned into a red cloak, caught up at the shoulder with a Celtic brooch. Leather thongs were wound around his woollen trousers, emphasising the strong muscles of his legs. He even seemed to have grown in stature.

'You look... you look different, Baldur,' said Finn in awe.

Baldur grinned, his overbite now really visible. 'That's because it's near my time, lad,' he said. 'This is my last earthly appearance. Whatever happens after tonight, for good or evil, I will never be seen like this again. And see?' He stepped into the candlelight. 'I can tolerate light. That certainly makes a change from a thousand years of gloom.'

'Nice brooch,' said Tara, noticing the piece of jewellery shining in the light.

Baldur put his hand to the brooch.

'That was given to me before my last battle,' he said.

'By Áine?' said Tara.

Baldur nodded.

'Aaahhh,' said Tara. 'Was she lovely?'

Baldur nodded. 'Beautiful. Tall and slender with long auburn hair. She used to come to where I trained my warriors. I can still see her standing there, hair blowing in the wind and her two wolfhounds by her side. "Noisy hounds," she called them, but they would do anything for her.' He sighed. 'If only...' he began. There was a faraway look on his ghostly face.

'No "if only",' said Tara, jumping into action. 'Listen, I'll go and look for something a bit fancy to spread on the raft. Wouldn't want you meeting your loved one without the proper trimmings.'

Finn continued to stare at his warrior friend. Baldur took Finn's hand and placed it on his chest. Under the wool tunic, Finn could feel a heartbeat.

'Jeez!' he breathed. 'You're alive!'

Baldur smiled. 'That's thanks to you,' he whispered. 'Your friendship and faith in me has made me strong again. I want you to be the last person to feel my heart before I go, Finn.'

In that instant, Finn felt a surge of courage, affection and loyalty course through his blood.

'I wish you didn't have to go,' he said.

'Ha!' laughed Baldur. 'A one-thousand-year-old Viking warrior is hardly a companion for a boy of your time. Besides, I doubt if there's much work for Masters of Arms in the twenty-first century. No,' he straightened himself up again. 'I must leave, Finn. You understand.'

Finn nodded. There was no need for words. The candles at the window spluttered, but by the time the startled trio glanced in that direction, the fleeting shadow that had caused the spluttering had passed.

The rats stirred. The Master! The Master had come. Soon now he would command them. They were ready.

Tara tossed a holey, discoloured lace tablecloth to Finn.

'Get that on to the raft,' she said. 'Am I the only one doing any work around here?' Then she rummaged in her rucksack and produced a stub of a pencil.

'Lip liner,' she said. 'Free with a magazine. It's the only thing I can find that will make a mark. Will it do?' She picked up a hand-sized stone from the floor and offered the two items to Baldur. There was a sigh of relief when the stone and the pencil stayed firmly in Baldur's hand.

'Funny,' said Tara.

'What's funny?' asked Baldur, looking at his now almost flesh-coloured hand.

'You're holding those in that spooky hand and your real hand is there.' She pointed to the skeletal hand.

Baldur shrugged. 'That's one of the mysteries of death, Tara,' he said.

'Come on,' put in Finn, glancing nervously at the window to make sure the candles were still burning brightly. 'It's getting late. What else for your funeral raft?'

'Something precious,' said Baldur. 'A bit of jewellery, perhaps.'

'Your brooch,' said Tara.

'I'm afraid not,' replied Baldur. 'I already have that. It has to be something specially given for the funeral pyre.'

Without hesitating, Finn took the watch from his wrist.

'Take this,' he said. 'This is precious.'

Tara glanced at him quizzically. But Finn just smiled. 'It's OK,' he said. 'I know exactly what I'm doing.' I know you'll understand, Mum. This is right. He carefully wound the blue Velcro strap around the twig-like bunch of bones that had once been Baldur's hand and laid it on the raft. 'Anything else?' he looked at Baldur.

'Well, there was usually food,' Baldur said. 'I can't think why, there's not much desire to eat when you've passed over. But that's how it was at Viking funerals. Food for the journey into the next life, they said.'

'We're fresh out of wild boar,' said Tara. 'But would a couple of squares of chocolate do?'

'I've never tasted it,' said Baldur. 'But if you say it is good, then I will abide by that. Now,' he went on, 'there's just one more thing to make a chieftain's funeral pyre complete.'

'Sticks to light it?' said Finn. 'We have loads of those. See? Wood shavings and offcuts of timber.'

Baldur was shaking his head. 'A female slave,' he said. 'We used to sacrifice a female slave and put her on the raft.'

There was a stunned silence. But even in that momentary silence, none of them heard the soft shuffling across the yard as the rats began to flow towards the shed.

'You've got to be kidding,' said Tara. 'That's really gross.'

'That's how it was,' said Baldur. 'It was optional, really. But it certainly added to a chief's heroic image.'

Tara began to laugh. 'Female slaves? Huh! If you weren't from the dark ages I'd have to thump a bit of sense into you, Baldur. Well, you'll have to kiss that part of your ceremony goodbye.'

'Hold on,' put in Finn. 'Would a symbol do, Baldur? Not a real female, but something that looks like a female?'

Baldur looked puzzled. 'A symbol of a woman? I don't understand, Finn.'

Finn dashed across to where Tara had put her old Sindy doll on top of a cabinet the day before.

'Here you are,' Finn laughed. 'Bit grubby, but she's pretty much a female. You don't mind, do you Tara?' he looked at Tara for approval. She smiled.

'Well it's better than me, I suppose. Since I'm the only other female around. Besides, the tatty hair is pretty much like your own, Baldur, so you're well suited.'

While Tara and Finn laid all the items solemnly on the torn lace tablecloth which Tara had spread on the wood chips, Baldur set about drawing his runes on the small stone with the lip liner. When he was finished, he placed it beside the Sindy doll.

Finn and Tara peered at the angular letters which were surrounded by curvilinear patterns.

'It's a bit like Celtic design,' observed Tara. 'Your lot probably nicked our sort of designs. What does it say?'

Baldur drew himself up to his full height. 'It says, "This is the rune of Baldur, son of Bjorn of Norway, Master of Arms to Phelim O'Brien, Chieftain of all the O'Briens of Munster. May the spirit of Baldur be united with Áine, daughter of O'Brien, for all time in Valhalla to live in peace, love and tranquillity".'

'Oh, that's lovely, Baldur,' sighed Tara. 'Dead romantic.'

Finn looked at Tara's watch. 'Twenty to twelve,' he said. 'It's time to place Baldur's head on the raft and get down to the lake. Then we'll wrap some rags and papers around sticks and hope they'll stay alight long enough to get us that far. After that...' he shrugged.

'After that there's not much they can do to us, is there?' said Tara. She was trying to sound brave, but her nervousness came across clearly.

Finn opened the chest and carefully lifted the head. The sudden screeching and scrabbling made them all jump. The window rattled and the barricade shook.

'They're back,' gasped Finn. 'The rats are back! We've got to make those flaming torches—'

Tara screamed when there was a thunderous roar over their heads and the roof resounded with heavy pounding. The candles spluttered. The ones nearest the door and around the window were extinguished, causing new shadows to darken the corners. Finn and Tara instinctively clutched one another and shrank towards the back of the shed. Baldur stood before them protectively.

'Lua,' he whispered. 'He has come for me.'

CHAPTER NINETEEN

Now there was another sound.

'Listen!' cried Finn. Above the pounding and frantic scrabbling, a shrill wind was screaming around outside. Through the window the bushes swayed in eerie silhouettes against the navy blue night sky. But their macabre dance lasted only seconds before they were eclipsed by the rats that piled up once more, their claws scratching the glass. A pane shattered and several slithering bodies got through. Baldur grabbed the lance from his funeral raft.

'Quickly,' he shouted to the two youngsters, 'block off that gap.'

With his old instinct as a hunter-warrior in full swing, Baldur swiftly disposed of the rats that had got in, while Tara and Finn scrambled up to the window. Tara pressed a piece of wood to the hole which Finn nailed to the window frame.

'Should have done this before,' he panted.

'We thought we were rid of them,' said Tara, fighting against the pressure on the wood she was holding. 'We thought the light was making it safe for us.'

Finn hammered every bit of wood they could find into the window frame.

'It won't hold them for long,' he said. 'But it gives us a bit extra time.'

'Time for what?' asked Tara. 'We're trapped, Finn.'

Finn said nothing. There was no answer to Tara's question. Was this it? Were they destined to die here in an isolated shed, their bodies to be found next morning beside a raft laid out with a skull, a grubby Sindy doll and a skeletal hand with a classy watch on it? Tara's folks would have some job trying to reason with that lot, he thought. Before they died themselves, that is. If tonight goes wrong Baldur will lose everything he's waited one thousand years for, and Tara's family will be cursed. And I'll be dead.

'What can we do, Baldur?' he cried out against the horrifying sounds.

But Baldur said nothing. He just stood resolute, his arms spread behind him to enclose Finn and Tara in a protective embrace. The ghost had completely metamorphosed into a true combatant, poised and in charge. The passionate surge of fighting evil coursed through his body, thanks to a young boy with teeth like his, and a feisty girl. He was determined to protect them, just as he had protected Phelim O'Brien and Áine all those years ago.

The few remaining candles were casting eerie shadows as they flickered against the draught from the wind outside. Baldur tensed.

Tara screamed again when she heard more glass break underneath the boards. Finn pulled her to him. It won't be long now, Mum. Baldur picked up the lance again and watched the window. Petrified, Tara and Finn watched with him. Then Finn looked around for a weapon. No point in standing idly by. Besides, the action might stop the shivering that had taken over his body. And it wasn't from the cold. Tara, realising what he was looking for, tugged at his arm and nodded towards the long box that housed the croquet set.

'Just the thing,' she whispered, making her way over to it. Finn gave a sigh when she opened it and took out two chipped but sturdy mallets.

'Good on you,' he whispered back. 'You stay here to tackle any that get past us, OK? Rearguard action it's called.'

Tara nodded. She knew he was really trying to protect her, to keep her back from the impending breakthrough. But she was too weary and scared to argue. Then, clutching the mallet so tightly that his knuckles were white, Finn softly went to stand beside Baldur. The sharp crack of breaking glass cut through the other sounds. Now the wood was splintering. The first small, tearing claws appeared. So many of them, thought Finn, swallowing hard.

'Now!' said Baldur. With lance and croquet mallet, ghost and boy laid into the squealing creatures. Stepping over the bodies that fell at his feet, Finn kept pace with Baldur. Don't think of them as creatures. These things are more than just rats, they are an evil enemy and they must be stopped. He screamed his hatred as he struck. He could feel the sweat running into his eyes, but there was no time to wipe it away. And no time to see if Tara was all right. Just Tara. Keep Tara's face in focus in your mind, not her family. Protect Tara. Time. Bloody time. It must be close to midnight. Hopeless. Still they kept coming. Was there no end to the army of rats from Cluain na nGall? Now Tara was standing beside him. She was shouting as she swung her mallet, all weariness gone. Finn wanted to shout at her to go back, but he knew, even in these awful circumstances, that you didn't argue with Tara. Baldur glanced at the two youngsters battling beside him. What he was about to say was cut short by a sound that filled him and the other two with terror.

'Laughing!' cried Finn. 'It sounds like someone laughing!'

'He's toying with us, the evil monster,' murmured Baldur. 'He knows we're powerless.' It took him just a moment to make a decision. He threw down his lance. 'Stop!' he shouted.

Finn and Tara looked at him in amazement.

'Don't give up, Baldur,' Finn panted. 'Not now.'

But Baldur held up his hand. 'Lua!' he called out. 'It's me you want. Stop your evil guardians. I'll come to you.'

He moved towards the barricaded door. The rats stopped. There was a moment of absolute silence. Then the shed trembled, as if an earthquake had struck. This was followed by a low roar that seemed to come up from the ground and encompass the whole shed. Tara and Finn clapped their hands to their ears. There were just two candles still alight and these began to flicker. Baldur stood firm against all this. Then he turned towards Tara and Finn. The look of sadness on his face made Finn run to him. He pulled at the Viking's cloak.

'No, Baldur. You mustn't stop! We can do it. There's still time!' he shouted. But Baldur gently pushed the boy away.

. 'No, Finn,' he said. 'I must face my own enemy.' He turned away. 'Lua!' he called again.

'What about... what about Tara and her family?' Finn pleaded in a low voice so that Tara wouldn't hear. 'If Lua wins?'

'That's why I must fight him,' whispered Baldur. 'It's the only chance we have.'

Finn took a deep breath. He was terrified of what his ghostly friend would meet out in the open, but he knew that it was the only way. He and Tara had reached the end of their commitment. Now Baldur must take over. He nodded, pushed out his jaw to try and grit his teeth. One quick embrace. Tara stayed apart, sensed the special moment between the boy and the ghost.

'You must stay here,' Baldur went on, raising his voice against the dreadful rumblings. 'No matter what you see or hear, you must stay in the shed. You'll be safe here. Light those candles again. Keep them alight.'

Tara nodded miserably. She knew Baldur was right.

'Barricade this after me,' he said.

The earth-shaking rumbling got even louder.

'Baldur!' Tara shouted desperately.

'He has to do it this way, Tara,' cried Finn. 'We're no match for whatever is out there.'

Baldur reached the door and turned one last time, nodded and then set about taking away the barricade.

Tara covered her mouth with her hand. Finn tried even harder to grit his teeth and fight back his emotions and fears.

The gust of wind that whistled through the open door sent an icy chill around the shed. Without a backward glance Baldur went through. The roaring stopped. The sudden silence was thick with foreboding. Without waiting for Finn, Tara rushed to replace the barricade.

'Come on!' she shouted to the hopelessly drained Finn. 'Help me.'

Finn was still clutching his croquet mallet. But he knew that it would be useless now. The horror had gone way beyond croquet mallets and flaming torches. He went to help Tara. Then, leaving her to light more candles, he ran to the window. Outside he could see that the rats had formed a semicircle around the shed.

'They're still there!' he cried. 'The rats. They're making sure we don't get out!'

Tara ran to his side. She recoiled when she saw the menacing multitude facing the shed.

'Oh, God!' she muttered. 'Where's Baldur?'

'Look,' said Finn, fear in his voice.

From the darkest part of the yard, a heavy presence was frighteningly discernible in the moonlight. No form, no features, just an undulating manifestation of indescribable horror. Baldur was walking resolutely towards it.

'I am ready for you now, Lua,' Tara and Finn heard him cry out. 'I don't have my back to you like before. Face me.'

With that, he walked towards the dark shape. Finn jumped down from the window.

'I've got to help him!' he screamed.

As if in answer to that, Tara saw the rats close in on the shed.

'No good, Finn,' she cried. 'They're waiting to pounce on us if we so much as open the door. We're trapped.'

Finn gave a desperate groan and climbed back beside her. Risking the rats attacking the window, they moved the candles to the table behind them, the better to see out. The rats didn't attack, they maintained their menacing watch, glittering eyes focused on the youngsters.

'I should've gone with him,' muttered Finn.

'To do what?' said Tara. 'This stuff is way out of our league, Finn.'

They watched helplessly as Baldur confronted the evil shadow, still holding his lance. His sudden movement made the youngsters jump. Now Baldur was twisting in and out of the dark.

'Baldur!' shouted Finn.

The rats moved closer to the shed, teeth bared in warning.

'Oh lord!' exclaimed Tara. 'He's going to die again.'

Time after time the silent battle flashed in the shadows, Baldur's scarlet cloak swirling in and out like the rinsing of a red-laden paintbrush in black water. Then, in response to a deep roar from the twisting mass, the rats suddenly turned to converge on the place where Baldur was struggling.

'That's not fair!' yelled Tara. 'Baldur's almost human, they'll finish him!'

The humped backs slithered noiselessly across the yard in obedience to their master. In a matter of seconds, Baldur would be totally immersed under their slimy bodies. 'We've lost, Finn,' she went on, sliding to the floor because she could no longer bear to watch. 'Lua will keep fighting until past midnight. Then he'll have won.'

Finn gave a start. It wasn't yet midnight! He looked down at Tara, his face shining with determination.

'That's it!' he hissed. 'Now's our chance! Those toerag rats aren't watching us.'

'You mean we should run?' asked Tara.

'The raft!' Finn whispered.

He didn't need to say more. Tara nodded and jumped up. Without another word, they quietly eased the barricade from the door. With a quick check to see that everything else was in place, Finn once more picked up the skull of Baldur and placed it on the moth-eaten cushion. Then, picking up the raft, they extinguished the last couple of candles so that the light wouldn't flood through the open door. With breath held, they slipped out. Keeping in the shadows, they made their way towards the lake.

'Concentrate on doing this,' Finn hissed when he saw Tara's attention begin to waver as she looked fearfully towards the stormy sounds in the shadows behind. 'Don't even look. Switch all that's going on out of your mind. This is what matters.'

Tara nodded and kept her vision focused on the lake, shimmering in the summer night sky. The water rippled softly around their ankles as they lowered their burden into the water. Finn stood up and breathed a sigh of relief.

'Time?' he asked.

Tara peered at the luminous digits on her watch.

'Four minutes to twelve,' she breathed. 'Have you matches?'

Finn pulled a box from his pocket and waved it at her.

'Go on, then. Do it!'

Finn struck a match. It sparked for a moment and went out.

'Dammit!' he swore, pulling out another one. He struck it, cupped it in his hand and set it among the wood shavings on the raft. He and Tara held their breath again until the small glow became a flame. With a comforting crackle the offcuts of wood picked up the flame and it began to spread over the raft.

'Now push,' Finn called. Between them they thrust the fiery raft further into the lake, not caring that the cold water was up to their waists. Finn ignored the swishing sound in the reeds behind him, dismissed it as a night breeze. But there was no breath of wind on the lake. It was Tara who glanced behind. What she saw made her stumble in the water, every nerve tense with yet more terror.

'Oh no!' she shrieked. 'They've seen us!'

Finn turned. In the glow from the gathering flames he was horrified to see the mass of rats descend on the lake. The churning water was coming towards the horrified youngsters. Now and then a head broke the surface, only to go under the surface of the water again as its eyes reflected the gathering flames.

'Push!' shouted Finn. 'Don't let them get to the raft, Tara.'

'I'm trying,' came the muffled reply.

The bodies of the rats buffeted horribly against the youngsters again and again as they congregated underneath the raft, away from the firelight. Wet, slimy bodies against wet clothes. The raft began to rock.

'They're trying to turn it!' Finn cried. 'They're trying to put out the fire!'

He and Tara held fast to keep the raft upright, but the weight of the rats was pulling it out of their control.

Any second now and the whole thing would capsize, extinguishing the precious flames and tossing Baldur's bones into the muddy water.

'I can't hold on any longer,' cried Tara, falling backwards into the inky lake and spluttering as the water splashed into her mouth. 'We're almost out of our depth.'

Sobbing with frustration, Finn clung to the raft with one hand, shielding his face from the flames with the other. But he could see that they were no match for the hordes of rats. His face was now level with the side of the raft and he was out of his depth. The fire reflected off the wet fur of a couple of rats that were now on the raft at Finn's eye level. Scouts, not bothered by the light, they turned their snarling faces towards him. 'Get away!' he roared. They don't kill. Scouts don't kill. Baldur said so. Teeth bared, they slithered towards his grasping fingers. But they bite! Instinctively Finn pulled his hand away and watched helplessly as the raft floated out of his reach. He swam over to Tara. Together they watched the flames dance as the raft rocked higher and higher, like a creature in its final throes of death.

Tara gave a sob of hopelessness and leaned on Finn's shoulder.

Suddenly a sharp, female voice broke into the night. 'Seek!' it shouted.

Tara and Finn turned. At the edge of the lake they could just make out the shadowy figure of a woman.

Something on the raft caused a single flame to burn brighter and higher. It was just for a moment, but it was long enough for the youngsters to see an image of a tall, slender woman with flowing hair and a long dress that rippled in the breeze. On either side of her stood two massive dogs. At her command the two dogs charged into the water.

'Wolfhounds!' exclaimed Tara, clutching on to Finn as they struggled towards the shallower water. 'Are they wolfhounds?'

'I can't see,' replied Finn. 'But they're big.'

The creatures were concealed by their own splashing in the dark water, but they passed near enough for him to hear their panting breath.

'Look!' cried Tara, grabbing some reeds to pull herself up. 'Oh, Finn. Look!' She reached out and pulled Finn beside her. Around the flaming raft there was a furore of thrashing and screeching. Tara and Finn gasped when they saw, silhouetted against the flames, the bodies of the rats as they were tossed into the air. Then everything went quiet. The raft continued its journey towards the centre of the lake. The flames danced higher into the dark sky, sending out sparks like miniature fireworks.

Then, from across the lake, came the familiar whirr of the church clock clearing its throat before launching into its midnight chiming.

'My God! We did it!' whispered Finn. 'Baldur's funeral pyre. We did it, Tara.'

Did he imagine it, but did some white plumes of smoke take the form of a smiling face with a distinct overbite? And was it joined by another form, also smiling, of a woman with flowing hair? Less than a second. Too fleeting to really register on the eye.

'Nah. Imagination,' he murmured, half to himself.

'I saw it too,' said Tara, 'it wasn't imagination.'

They watched for another few moments until the fire diminished and fizzled out.

'Let's go,' said Finn, shivering. 'It's cold.'

As they turned to wade ashore, two bounding shapes splashed towards them from the deeper water. Tara and Finn froze. Not more weird stuff. Please. No more. Finn felt all his remaining strength ebb away. No adrenaline left.

'It's Ben and Bella!' exclaimed Tara.

Sure enough, the two small dogs paddled up beside them.

'That pair?' said Finn, glancing back to where the recent battle had taken place in the water. 'I thought they were two bigger dogs.'

'Wolfhounds,' said Tara. 'I could have sworn they were big Irish wolfhounds.'

'Come on, you two,' shouted a commanding female voice from the shore. 'You'll catch your death of cold.'

'Granny Dob!' cried Tara. 'It's Granny Dob.'

Mrs Cavendish helped the two youngsters from the muddy water.

'I thought I heard a commotion,' she said.

But, for some reason, she didn't ask any questions.

CHAPTER TWENTY

Finn lay in bed and studied the sunlit walls of his bedroom, figuring where he'd put his old movie posters. He'd ask Meg for some Blu-Tack and put them up later. He swung his legs over the bed and rummaged in his bag for a clean T-shirt. He paused, looked at the messy bundle of clothes in the bag, then shoved them into the chest of drawers. He threw the empty bag on top of the wardrobe.

Downstairs Meg was scraping the remains of breakfast into the bin. She looked up when Finn came in, unsure of what to say. But Finn gave her a friendly nod.

'Hi,' he said, going to the cupboard to help himself to cereal.

'You're all right then?' said Meg.

'I'm fine,' replied Finn, smiling at her concerned face. 'Really fine.'

'We were so... so...'

'Gobsmacked?' said Finn.

Meg nodded. 'Gobsmacked. Me and Bill were so gobsmacked when you arrived here with Mrs Cavendish in the early hours of the morning, and you in borrowed clothes. We were so worried when we came back late and found the front door unlocked. And then Bill went to your room. We thought you'd...' she hesitated.

'You thought I'd bunked off?' said Finn. 'Run away? Ha! Fat chance. You won't get rid of me that easily. You're stuck with me now.'

Meg smiled and began loading the dishes into the dishwasher. She looked almost shyly at Finn as she shook the detergent into the compartment on the door.

'Is it true what she said, about the rats, I mean?'

'Yep,' said Finn, spooning sugar over his cereal. 'I knew where the nest was.'

'My goodness,' Meg was shaking her head. 'And yourself and that young girl got rid of them. I still can't understand.'

'Don't try, Meg,' laughed Finn. 'It's all over. There won't be any more rats.'

'Well, that's a relief then,' said Meg. 'That Mrs Cavendish kept on and on about how brave you were.'

Finn waved his hand dismissively. 'Oh, let's forget it,' he said. 'Did you know,' he went on, diverting Meg's attention away from himself, 'that Mrs Cavendish's name was Deirdre O'Brien before she married – that's where her nickname, Dob, comes from, D.O.B. see? Back in the time of Brian Boru her ancestor was a chieftain here. His name was Phelim O'Brien.'

'No, I didn't know that,' said Meg, wondering what on earth it was all about, but pleased that Finn was sharing this with her.

'Imagine being able to trace your family back that far,' went on Finn.

Meg shrugged. 'We all have ancestors,' she said, closing the door of the dishwasher and setting the controls. 'We all go back to someone whose genes we've inherited, whether we know who they were or not.'

Finn's spoon stopped halfway to his mouth. Then he smiled and continued eating.

Later, as he crossed the yard, he met Bill carrying the new lamb into the morning sunshine. Finn stopped to look.

'Will it be OK?' he asked.

Bill laughed and rubbed the lamb's head. 'He'll do just great. He'll have to be bottle-fed for a while, but the sunshine will make him strong.'

Finn reached out and gingerly patted the small creature.

'I have a friend,' he began hesitantly. 'Could I... do you think I could bring her over and show her this fellow?'

Bill wrinkled his nose. 'Don't know about that,' he said, shaking his head.

Finn looked at him in surprise.

'Girls,' went on Bill. 'Give him a silly name and want to put ribbons round his neck. Start shampooing the poor thing. Make him feel a right wally.'

Finn grinned when he realised Bill was kidding.

'Maybe in your day,' he said. 'But not this girl. Not Tara. She'll like him just as he is.'

'Oh, go on then,' said Bill.

He stood and watched Finn break into a run as he went towards the avenue.

'A girlfriend, huh?' he muttered to the lamb. 'Have to watch our p's and q's now, won't we, fella?'

Tara was waiting for Finn when he reached their usual meeting place on the hill.

'Did you sleep?' she asked him.

'Not a lot,' replied Finn. 'Too excited. Too much going on in my head.'

'Me too,' said Tara. 'But, the thing is, we did it, you and me. We're fantastic, aren't we?'

Finn grinned. 'Too right. We gave Baldur as fine a sendoff as he could have wished for.'

'Come on,' said Tara, grabbing his arm. 'Let's go to where that... that battle took place last night. See if there was any ghostly blood spilt.'

Finn hesitated.

'Oh, come on,' went on Tara. 'After last night we can face anything. Anyway, we have to fix up our shed. I've got a mini-charcoal thing that Granny Dob gave me. She said we can have barbecues there – ask other kids from around, so they'll get to know you before school starts.'

Finn's thumb instinctively went towards his teeth. But he folded his arms instead.

As they neared the circle of trees around the Viking plot, Finn froze when he heard a rumble.

Tara laughed. 'Machines,' she said, pulling him along.

They stood and watched for a while. The heavy diggers were tearing into the grass and lifting great gigantic scoops of earth. Men with yellow helmets were outlining what appeared to be sites with white string.

'That's it, then,' said Tara. 'No more Viking bones. Just a load of noisy tourists.'

Finn said nothing, just stood and stared at the work that was going on.

'Finn?' said Tara. 'Are you sad to see all this? Maybe we shouldn't have come this way. What are you thinking?'

But Finn was smiling. 'I'm thinking that Baldur may be delighted with what's going on,' he said.

'Yeah?'

'Definitely. No more lumpy battlefield, just a bunch of folks enjoying holidays. He'd like that.'

'I suppose you're right,' said Tara. She looked up into the sky. 'Valhalla. Where do you think Valhalla is, Finn?'

Finn shook his head. 'Haven't a clue.' Then, with a mischievous gleam in his eyes he said, 'How do we know if it even exists?'

Tara looked at him scornfully. 'How can you say that? As if all we did was for nothing! What a miserable thought.' She looked up to the sky again. 'I certainly believe that they're somewhere up there, Baldur and Áine, hand in hand in a gorgeous place...' She broke off when she saw the mischief in Finn's eyes. 'You creep, you've been winding me up. You do believe they are. I know you do.'

Finn laughed and ran ahead.

Apart from the mess in the shed, there wasn't much evidence of last night's awful events. They tentatively approached the spot where the couple of one-thousand-year-old adversaries had raged in battle the night before. The spot near the laurels had just a few leaves scattered about, as if blown off their branches by a strong wind. Tara was disappointed.

'Thought we might find bits of that scummy Lua,' she said, kicking the earth with her toe. 'Anyway, how do we know who won?'

Finn looked at her with mock scorn.

'Whose funeral pyre did we succeed in sending through the lake?' he asked.

'Baldur's,' replied Tara.

'And what time was that?'

'Midnight.'

'So?'

Tara laughed. 'So Baldur won. I knew that – just testing.'

'There y'are then,' went on Finn. 'No need to look for evidence. While Baldur kept that murdering prat busy, we did our bit.'

'I wonder if he knew we'd do what we did,' mused Tara.

'More than likely,' replied Finn. Oh yes, he thought. Baldur knew I'd be with him to the end. He knew I'd see him through. We goofy warriors stick by one another. He didn't have to ask. He knew.

They stood at the doorway of the shed and looked in at the chaos of scattered junk.

'Never mind,' said Tara. 'We'll fix it up even better than before.'

Finn went over to the chest where Baldur's skull had lain. Tara stole a sly look at him, trying to gauge what he was feeling. Being Tara, upfront and candid, she had to ask.

'You miss the old ghoul, don't you?'

She didn't make any comment when Finn responded by pushing his thumb under his teeth.

'I suppose,' he said, examining the bite mark, just like he always did when he was thinking. 'I'd have liked more time to say goodbye.'

'Oh, what's the point in long goodbyes?' said Tara. 'They're schmaltzy and sentimental. Shake hands, kissy kissy – no way! Isn't it better to remember Baldur going to do battle with that creep Lua? That way you'll always think of him as a tough warrior.'

'Maybe,' said Finn. He looked into the chest where Baldur's head had been. 'Hey!' he exclaimed.

'What?' Tara came running over. 'Don't tell me his head's back.'

'No,' said Finn, holding up something. 'Look.'

'Baldur's brooch!' said Tara. 'It must have fallen off in the fight. Maybe he'll come back for that and you'll see him again.'

'No,' said Finn. 'He's gone for good this time. A bit of jewellery isn't going to be of much interest to him. Not now that he's got everything he needs.'

The yapping from outside made them both jump. Ben and Bella charged in, jumping at Tara and Finn's knees.

'I thought I'd find you here,' said Mrs Cavendish, pushing some of the junk out of her way.

'Look what we've found,' said Tara, pointing to the brooch Finn was holding.

Mrs Cavendish took it from Finn and examined it, squinting because she didn't have her glasses.

'I recognise this,' she said.

Finn's heart sank. Was it just another bit of discarded rubbish after all, and not Baldur's brooch?

'There are pictures of this in the family annals,' went on Mrs Cavendish. 'There were several of these handed down from generation to generation for hundreds of years. Most of them got lost eventually. It's the O'Brien brooch.'

'I totally forgot your name used to be O'Brien, Granny Dob,' put in Tara.

Mrs Cavendish looked at her granddaughter with an exaggerated gesture of exasperation. 'But you've always said ancestors are boring, dear. You've never really wanted to hear my stories of family matters, have you?'

Tara rolled her eyes to heaven and grinned at Finn. 'Just about the battle,' she said. 'I remembered what you said about the battle. That was interesting. The rest just passed me by.'

Mrs Cavendish smiled and shook her head. Then she ran her fingers over the delicate design. 'Very beautiful.'

'Well, lucky I found it then,' said Finn. 'Now you can put it with the rest of your family heirlooms.'

Mrs Cavendish looked at him with an intensity that made him nervous. Finn put it down to a trick of the light, but for just a second her eyes seemed to be the eyes of a younger woman. She held the brooch for another moment, then reached out and handed it to Finn, shaking her head as she did so.

'No,' she said gently. 'I do believe that this belongs to you, Finn.'

As if in a trance, Finn took the brooch. She knows. Something way inside her head from all those generations, has connected. As he clasped the brooch he felt closer to Baldur than he could ever put into words. He watched Mrs Cavendish as she made her way out of the shed.

'Come, dogs,' she said to Ben and Bella. 'Noisy hounds.'

'So now,' said Tara. 'Somewhere out there Baldur has something precious belonging to you, and here you've got something precious belonging to him. Neat, eh?'

Finn squeezed the brooch tightly. A fair exchange, Mum.

'Listen to that machinery in the distance,' said Tara. 'The Cavendish curse is finished at last.'

Finn turned to her with amazement. 'You knew about it, then? The curse?'

Tara looked puzzled. 'What are you on about, you daft thing? The only curse on my family was lack of dosh.

And now we have that, thanks to the sale of Cluain na nGall. Just think, no more charity shop gear and old mutton stews.'

Finn laughed. 'You? Charity shop? I don't think so. You never.'

'Well, it sounds better when you stick in a bit of a contrast, like letting go an old way of life for a new way, doesn't it?'

Finn laughed again. 'You're mental,' he said. 'You talk in riddles.'

But then he thought about what Tara had said.

'Ha,' he said. 'You're right, Tara. I can live with that.'